**The instant he h
something in hi…
trying to keep at…**

He'd known Katherine an hour, tops, and his heart ached from a fear that came from knowing what could have happened to her out in the storm. That fear caught at his middle and made him hold her even tighter. This woman with the incredible green eyes was threatening the foundation of his carefully constructed new life.

Fear. Real fear. It was hash and unwelcome. "What in the hell were you thinking?" he demanded with more roughness than he intended. "I told you to stay in the truck. That I'd be back."

"Looking for…you," she said in a voice so unsteady and low that he almost couldn't make out her words.

He held her away from him and saw her chin trembling. "You could have been seriously hurt."

"Oh, Mac," she gasped. "I thought…" She shuddered violently. "I never meant…"

He knew then that once Katherine left, being alone would never feel right again.

Dear Reader,

Things get off to a great start this month with another wonderful installment in Cathy Gillen Thacker's series THE DEVERAUX LEGACY. In *Their Instant Baby*, a couple comes together to take care of an adorable infant—and must fight *their* instant attraction. Be sure to look for a brand-new Deveraux story from Cathy when *The Heiress*, a Harlequin single title, is released next March.

Judy Christenberry is also up this month with a story readers have been anxiously awaiting. Yes, Russ Randall does finally get his happy ending in *Randall Wedding*, part of the BRIDES FOR BROTHERS series. We also have *Sassy Cinderella* from Kara Lennox, the concluding story in her memorable series HOW TO MARRY A HARDISON. And rounding out things is *Montana Miracle*, a stranded story with a twist from perennial favorite Mary Anne Wilson.

Next month begins a yearlong celebration as Harlequin American Romance commemorates its twentieth anniversary! We'll have tons of your favorite authors with more of their dynamic stories. And we're also launching a brand-new continuity called MILLIONAIRE, MONTANA that is guaranteed to please. Plus, be on the lookout for details of our fabulous and exciting contest!

Enjoy all we have to offer and come back next month to help us celebrate twenty years of home, heart and happiness!

Sincerely,

Melissa Jeglinski
Associate Senior Editor
Harlequin American Romance

MONTANA MIRACLE
Mary Anne Wilson

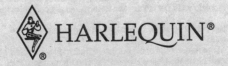

HARLEQUIN®

TORONTO • NEW YORK • LONDON
AMSTERDAM • PARIS • SYDNEY • HAMBURG
STOCKHOLM • ATHENS • TOKYO • MILAN • MADRID
PRAGUE • WARSAW • BUDAPEST • AUCKLAND

For my dad, Herb Bignell
My hero
I miss you

ISBN 0-373-16952-3

MONTANA MIRACLE

Copyright © 2002 by Mary Anne Wilson.

This edition published by arrangement with Harlequin Books S.A.

® and TM are trademarks of the publisher. Trademarks indicated with
® are registered in the United States Patent and Trademark Office, the
Canadian Trade Marks Office and in other countries.

Visit us at www.eHarlequin.com

Printed in U.S.A.

ABOUT THE AUTHOR

Mary Anne Wilson is a Canadian transplanted to Southern California, where she lives with her husband, three children and an assortment of animals. She knew she wanted to write romances when she found herself "rewriting" the great stories in literature, such as *A Tale of Two Cities*, to give them "happy endings." Over a ten-year career, she's published more than thirty romances, had her books on bestseller lists, been nominated for Reviewer's Choice Awards and received a Career Achievement Award in Romantic Suspense. She's looking forward to her next thirty books.

Books by Mary Anne Wilson

HARLEQUIN AMERICAN ROMANCE

*Just For Kids

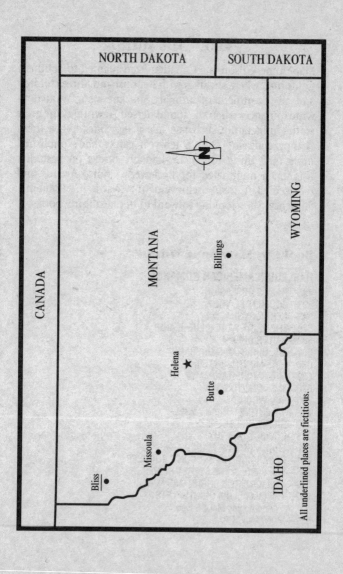

Prologue

He looked around the party in the glass-and-steel house high in the Hollywood Hills and saw nothing but emptiness. The women and men, partying as if there were no tomorrow, didn't exist for him at that moment. Nothing existed for him. Not even himself. Dr. Mackenzie Parish. That man was gone. Gone.

Mac set his champagne, untouched, on the marble table by massive glass doors opened to the terrace and the night beyond. A blanket of city lights lay far below, a city as unreal to him as he felt at that moment. He turned from it, pushed his hands into the pockets of his leather bomber jacket and headed for the spiral metal stairs that went down three flights to the garage level.

He was down two flights when he heard someone call out, "Doc? Hey, Doc!" the sound echoing off the stairwell walls, which were splashed with modern art.

He looked up, and on the top landing someone was waving to him. Clarisa? Marissa? He couldn't remember the name of the woman he'd met when he'd walked into the party less than an hour ago. An actress of some sort, he thought, although he'd never seen her in the movies. A woman who hung out at parties like this, a woman who did whatever it took to be close enough to fame to rub shoulders with it.

She hung over the railing, dangerously close to coming down without using the stairs. "Where you going?" she called, a bit tipsy now, no surprise, the way she'd been drinking champagne. Blond, busty, tattooed on one shoulder, a snake or something, poured into a dress a size too small. Pretty, if one looked at her with unprofessional eyes. But he could see where she'd been "nipped and tucked," and although it was done well, she wasn't anywhere near the twentysomething she was pretending to be.

"See you," he called out, and started down again.

"Hey, I'll go with you!"

He would have taken her up on the offer three months ago, but now he rejected it out of hand. If he'd still been Mac Parish, doctor to the stars, he would have motioned for her to come on down. She would have been thrilled to be with him. A genius at plastic surgery, a man who worked on the best and brightest, wealthy, famous in his own right. But he ignored her offer now and hurried out of her sight.

He reached the garage level, pushed open the outer door and met the valet, a man probably working as a valet while he waited to be "discovered." He was young and good-looking, obviously worked out and had a megawatt smile. "Ready to leave, sir?" he asked brightly.

"Yes." Mac handed him his tag and the guy nodded.

"Be right back, sir," he said as he set off.

Mac stood alone and took a breath. He must be real. He could feel the chilly October air rush into his lungs, could hear the drone of voices and the music drifting from the multistoried house. But he still didn't feel real. He took out his wallet for a tip to give the valet and stopped when he saw the only picture he carried in the slender leather holder.

It was a small photo of three people, a softly pretty woman, a sleeping baby in her arms, and a man in his early thirties. The man was Mac's mirror image. Almost a dead ringer, but the man in the picture had shorter hair, no razor cut, but just as thick and sandy blond. Hazel eyes squinted into bright sunlight, eyes set in a face with rugged features that seemed to be all planes and angles. His skin was tanned but not from sets of tennis in the California sun at private clubs. It was from hard work in the outdoors.

The look on the man's face was something Mac almost didn't remember ever feeling, the look of a man who had everything he ever wanted. The delicate blond woman at his side smiled at him as if he was the center of her world. The baby in her arms, swaddled in a blue blanket, linked them forever.

"You have nothing, Mac. You stopped existing a long time ago."

Mac shoved back the memory of those words as headlights arced up the driveway, blinding him for a moment. Then the low throb of the Porsche's engine vibrated in the air as the car slid to a stop in front of him. The valet got out and took the bill Mac offered him in exchange for the keys. Mac got in, and he drove down the winding driveway to the street below.

"You can't go on like this. I won't let you."

The words rang in his memory as he headed south toward Hollywood Boulevard. *"You're lost. You're so lost."*

He reached for his cell phone, hit a number and waited for two rings. A woman answered in a sleepy voice. "Yes?"

"It's me. I'm coming back. I'll be there tomorrow."

"We'll be waiting," she said.

Mac flipped the phone shut, tossed it on the empty passenger seat and took the last curve so fast that the tires of the sports car squealed on the pavement. When he reached the boulevard, he never looked back. He concentrated on what was ahead of him, and what he had to do.

"You're lost, so lost."

He was going to find Mac Parish. He wasn't sure he'd like what he found at the end of his search. But if he was going to try to find himself, that meant going back.

Chapter One

Katherine Ames stood in the cramped office of James Lowe, the features editor at the *Final Word,* a Los Angeles-based magazine that fed into the public's need to know anything and everything about celebrities and would-be celebrities. She was watching edited video on the largest of five television monitors set on the far wall. "Why am I watching this?" she asked, never looking away from the screen that showed arrivals of the stars and celebrities at a movie premiere.

"Watch, Kate, just watch." James said. Lights flashed, and a white limo drew up to the curb at the end of the red carpet. A banner scrolled across the bottom of the screen—*Dr. Mackenzie Parish*—at the same time James spoke again. "There he is."

The limo stopped and the door was opened. The scroll on the bottom of the screen changed to *The Doctor to the Stars* as the man himself stepped out onto the carpet and into a sea of lights, microphones and interviewers. Fans were held back by security guards and velvet ropes.

Kate had seen the doctor the way most of the public had, his face plastered all over the gossip pages, filling a lot of space in magazines like theirs, a man with as much "presence" as a lot of his clients, the beautiful and the famous. Now he was standing on the carpet, a tall, lean man, with sandy hair, in a well-tailored tuxedo, smiling, waving, offering his arm to his companion, a tall, leggy blonde with more hair than dress.

"Look at that guy. He had everything," James murmured.

Kate saw Parish turn and for a fraction of a second, he looked right at the camera. His dark eyes narrowed slightly at the glare from the lights. His face sharply angular with a strong jaw, he was clean-shaven and had just enough lines around his eyes and mouth to make him ruggedly appealing.

He was a striking man, attractive in a definitely male way, with a deep, even tan that set off the color of his longish hair, brushed straight back from his face. The blonde waved and giggled, holding on to his arm as if he were her personal trophy.

"Yeah, he had everything," Kate said, slightly taken aback when he smiled at the woman with him. A half smile, really, but enough to crinkle the skin at the corners of his eyes, lifting his lips in what was almost a seductive manner. The man was sexy. Damn sexy. He was listening to a bimbo starlet as if she was telling him the secret of life. Right then James paused the picture, freezing that frame, and the smile.

"He sure as hell did," James said. "Everything."

"Where's this going?" Kate asked, turning from

the image and feeling oddly uneasy. "This tape's at least two years old."

James was still looking at the monitor, and his pale-blue eyes, even paler in his deeply tanned face, narrowed thoughtfully. With his shock of blond hair styled to a T and his fashionably rumpled look, he definitely looked like a thirtysomething man on the way up. Any way he could get there.

James finally turned his gaze to Kate. "The question everyone's tried to answer is, why did he walk away right when he was at the top? He was the best nip-and-tuck man in the city, privy to the inner circle of this town. He had any woman he wanted. Why did he leave and go to some blip on a map in the middle of nowhere and drop out of sight?"

She shrugged. "Drugs, women, rock and roll? Malpractice, gambling? You name a vice, and I'm sure someone's thought about pegging him with it. But the fact is, no one's been able to peg anything on him, no matter how hard they try." She looked at James. "Are you saying you've got something on him?"

"There, finally a question. I was wondering if your famous curiosity was fading. The one thing that's always fascinated me about you is the way you keep at something until you have all the answers. That's why you're damn good at this business."

"You didn't answer my question."

He exhaled. "Actually, it's the same thing that makes it impossible to be around you for very long."

Right then she remembered why she'd stopped seeing James six months ago. He'd been just as impossible to be around for any length of time as she'd been for him. Any relationship between the two of them ended up being almost all business and no fun. "Same back at you," she murmured. "Now, answer my question. Do you have some new facts on this?"

"Facts? No, but I've got an idea." He studied her for a long moment, then said, "From where I'm sitting, I'm looking at someone with a brain who knows how to go for the jugular, a woman who is definitely the type the good doctor favors. A tall, leggy blonde."

"James, what the—"

"You heard me. You're a hell of a reporter and you've got that extra something that can make the difference. In this business, you know you need every edge you can get." Without warning he was out of his chair, coming around to take her by her arm.

He ignored the way she tried to get free of his hold and took her over to a mirrors. He got behind her and made her face the reflection.

"There. Look. You're what's going to make this happen." His hands rested on her shoulders, his fingers tightening slightly. "Everyone's tried everything and gotten nowhere. A cement wall. And I got to thinking, the man has to have a weakness, something that will get to him, and from everything I've seen, that weakness is beautiful blondes."

"I knew I broke up with you for some reason," she muttered.

"You also know I'm right," he said from right behind her. "Take a good look."

She stared at herself, at Katherine Ames, twenty-seven years old, tall, blond and leggy. That much was right. But at five feet ten inches, she was gangly. Her blond hair was very blonde, almost silvery, but straight and long and worn the way she had it now, in a single braid that ended halfway down her back. She wore little to no makeup, had freckles across her nose and what she thought was a very sharp chin.

She tended to wear what she had on then, simple slacks and a plain shirt, navy and white today. There were no tight miniskirts or plunging necklines, no bronzed skin, no big hair, and she had never been called voluptuous. She wasn't flat, but one of her dates had called her figure "boyish"—not the greatest compliment. No, she wasn't Parish's type, no matter what James thought.

"I'm not looking at some starlet bimbo," she said, meeting his gaze with a frown. "No makeup, no false lashes, no implants." She'd never thought of herself as beautiful. Rather, growing up as the only child of two selfish, self-centered people, had helped foster her strengths. She'd developed a fertile imagination to keep her occupied when she'd been alone, a desperate need to write so she could connect to something when she was by herself, and an insatiable curiosity about the outside world. Those were her credentials as a writer, what made her good at what she did, not any physical attributes. "I'm too thin, too tall and too pale, and I've got freckles."

James frowned at her over her shoulder. "Boy, your self-image is miserable," he said. "If you'd stop scowling like that and put on a bit of makeup, maybe let your hair loose, with those green eyes you'd stop traffic on Sunset Boulevard.''

She twisted around to face him and he drew back. ''If you want me to go after this story, give it to me.'' That familiar tingle of excitement was starting to grow in her at the challenge of getting to a subject and getting him or her to talk when no one else could. ''The thrill of the hunt,'' James had called it. ''If it's possible, I'll get it. But let me figure out what tack to use.''

''Hey, sure, absolutely.'' His pale eyes flicked suggestively over her, then he met her gaze again. ''You're a hell of a writer. I've always said that, and that's why you're here. So it's yours. Go for it.''

Even his compliments sounded compromising to her, but she wasn't going to take the bait that easily. ''Okay, give me details.''

He went back to his desk, reached for the folder and held it out to her. ''Here's everything we have.''

She crossed to take it from him, a thick manila folder with ''Dr. MacKenzie Parish'' in bold type on the right edge, then a list of names and dates on the cover, others who had checked it out of Research and the dates it had been in use. Lots of interest in the man. She opened the cover and shuffled through several glossies, magazine tear sheets and newspaper clippings.

Two of their own articles were mixed in with an impressive group of stories on the man. The headlines ran the gamut from Sexy Doc Nips & Tucks His Way To Fame, Partying Is A Science For This

Doctor, to Merry-Go-Round Stops For Famous Surgeon and The Doctor Has Left The Building.

And in every picture that wasn't a head-and-shoulders shot, he was with a woman. A star, a wanna-be star, a nobody. But always a beautiful woman. He definitely liked tall blondes. "He partied hard," she murmured, not bothering to hide her distaste for his lifestyle. She sank into the chair facing the desk, closing the folder and resting it in her lap. "So where is this place he ran off to?"

"Montana, a ranch outside the tiny town of Bliss, and from all accounts, he seldom leaves it."

"No favorite haunts, no daily schedule in here?" she asked, tapping the folder.

"Sorry, if it were that easy, someone would have done the story by now."

"Okay, there has to be a way to make him stick his head out of the bunker. Then the trick is to get him to talk."

He sat forward. "Getting him to talk is the easy part for you. You could get a monk to break a vow of silence. Look what you did with the Blanchard story." He smiled at her. "She wouldn't talk to anyone, and you got her to do an exclusive for us."

"That's different. I went to the same deli she did and saw her there all the time, and she recognized me."

"See what I mean? You use what you have to get what you want. Only you could turn a trip to the deli into a great interview with a woman who had just been acquitted of murdering her husband. You had an 'in' with her, and like it or not, you've got an 'in' with Parish.''

She hated it when he was right. But he was. If the man's weakness was blondes, she'd have to factor that into the equation, whatever she did. ''Bliss?'' she asked.

''Bliss as in a podunk town out in the middle of nowhere. Bliss for the gophers and cows, I guess.''

''Maybe for the doctor, too,'' she said.

''That's what you'll find out, won't you?'' he asked, stretching his arms over his head.

''I hope so.''

''Also, the bonus for an exclusive kicks in, and that can't hurt, either.''

She could use the money, but more than that, she loved this part of the job. The hunt, the discovery. She pressed her hand on the closed folder. ''What's the deadline?''

''I can give you a week, maybe a bit longer if it looks really good after you get there, but that's about all the budget will bear. Also, it'll give us time to make the semiannual special issue, too, if you come in around then.'' He took a thick envelope out of a side drawer. ''Here's your packet.''

She took it, and said, ''Okay, I'll give it a shot.''

''Just be prepared. From what's in the research, Bliss is a tight little community where the towns-people don't talk and won't even give directions to Parish's place.'' He tapped the envelope. ''That's what county assessors are for. There's a map in there of his place.'' He studied her. ''So, any ideas how to get to him?''

She didn't think, despite James's optimism about her looks, that putting on a skimpy silver dress and walking the streets would work. "Something will come to me. By the way, is there anyone living with him?" The man never seemed to be alone in L.A., so there was no reason to think he suddenly became a monk in Montana.

"No ranch hands this time of year, but there's a housekeeper, or a friend of some sort who keeps the house, and a little boy. Word is it's his dead brother's child, but there isn't a birth certificate on him in that county. Maybe the kid's his?" He glanced at the envelope. "You've got an air ticket for tomorrow out of LAX in there, car rental and your per diem. Sign off for the folder and read it on the plane." He scrounged around and passed her a pen.

As she signed the folder front and dated it, she asked, "What about a place to stay?"

"There're no hotels or motels listed in Bliss, but there's a bed-and-breakfast called Joanine's Inn. You're expected tomorrow evening by seven, under your own name. I wasn't sure about getting you a place to stay because of the holiday."

"Holiday?"

"Thanksgiving, Kate, remember?"

"I remember," she muttered.

"You come from a strange family, Kate. I've never heard of a family who ignores holidays the way yours do."

"They're a waste of time," she said, echoing her mother's words from years ago when she'd asked why they didn't do anything for Christmas. She'd stopped caring about holidays around the same time she stopped asking about them. "We never noticed them very much."

"By the way, how are Frank and Irene?"

"I haven't heard from them since…" She had to think about that one. Contact with her parents was rare. They left, and when they thought about it, they called. Kate was used to it. She'd been on her own since she was a teenager. "I guess it was in July sometime. They were in Borneo working on some irrigation project."

He sat back in the chair. "Fascinating people," he said. "Lousy parents."

She didn't argue with that. "They are what they are, and it's not important," she said, cutting off that discussion as she stood holding the folder and envelope.

"Kate?" he said when she would have left.

She turned to look at him. "Something else?"

"I'm not expecting miracles on this, but anything you can find I'll use."

She nodded and as she crossed to the door, she glanced at the still-frozen image on the monitor, the man and that smile. A real challenge. She tossed over her shoulder, "Keep that spot in the special open." She looked back at James before she went out the door. "Maybe the cover."

SNOW WAS BEAUTIFUL in pictures and on greeting cards, but that was the only experience Kate had ever had with the white stuff. She had no idea that in real life it could be blinding, even in the early evening, or that it could be driven by wind so hard that it shook a car and made it tremble, even though the car was a sturdy sedan she'd rented at the airport two hours before.

She had no concept of cold bone-chilling it penetrated the car windows while the heater fought fiercely to defeat it. Between cursing the weather and cursing herself for driving out here without checking the weather first, she maneuvered the car along the winding, hilly road that climbed into the Montana wilderness. The last sign for Bliss had said twenty miles, and the longer she drove, the more she thought a man like Dr. Parish couldn't possibly be anywhere near this godforsaken place.

The man was used to fast cars, luxury, pampering, leggy blondes. None of which would be out this way. At least not a leggy blonde with any sense at all. The idea made her laugh. She was beginning to feel like a dumb-blonde joke. She squinted at the road ahead. She was the punch line. All for a story. Then again, she would do just about anything for a good story. Her parents went to some primitive place to build water systems. She went to some primitive place for a story. She was more their daughter than she'd realized.

As she frowned at that thought, the car skidded slightly to the left. Before she could panic, it found traction again on the curve and settled on the road. Another sign for Bliss was caught in the headlights— ten more miles. She glanced at the clock on the dash. Five-thirty, yet it was so dark it might as well have been the middle of the night, and road visibility was almost nil.

The snow she'd driven into fifteen minutes ago had been falling in this area long enough to drift high on both sides of the highway. Now it was building up on the channel of the windshield wipers with each swipe.

She should have stopped at the first sign of snow and found a motel, then waited this out in warmth and safety. Parish wasn't going anywhere, but she'd been anxious to get to Bliss. That excitement for a new assignment had been building on the plane while she went over the Parish file in detail. Now she was convinced there was a dynamite story hidden in the Montana wilderness. Mac Parish hadn't just left: he'd gone into hiding.

Kate sensed it wasn't just a case of Mac's going back to his birthplace or being a glorified baby-sitter for the kid. He had no adult family left. Both parents were long gone and his only brother had died in an accident months ago. None of that added up to motivation for what he'd given up.

A house in Malibu on the cliffs over the ocean had been sold. His collection of sports cars was gone. His spot in the high-end cosmetic-surgery practice had been filled by another doctor within a month of his leaving. He wasn't coming back. He'd wiped out everything that would have brought him back.

The car skidded again on the icy road and seemed almost to float, as if the back of the car was about to trade places with the front. She hit the brakes at the same time she remembered reading that she shouldn't hit the brakes, but just steer into the slide. By the time she figured that out, it was too late.

The car spun the snowy road in a full circle, a slow-motion ballet of weirdness. Slowly, ever so slowly, it miraculously stopped dead in the center of the road and facing the right direction. Kate exhaled a shaky sigh of relief, until she realized that anyone who came around the corner was going to hit her. She was a sitting duck if she stayed there, but she was afraid to drive any farther.

She sat forward, swiping at the rapidly fogging windows. Beyond the laboring windshield wipers all she could see was the reflecting of the headlights in the snow.

She stretched to her right as far as the seat belt allowed to brush at the foggy side window. She was almost certain she could see a dark shadow out there, maybe ten feet away. A bank of snow? It had to be the side of the road. Carefully she inched the car toward it, until she was pretty sure she was off the main part of the road, then stopped.

She put on her flashers and sank back in the seat with relief. The heater was working while the car idled, and her clothes were keeping her snug enough. The corduroy jacket, shirt and jeans were fine, and her boots kept her feet warm. She could wait a bit, see if the snow let up and then go on to Bliss. Just wait. That was all she had to do.

She turned on the radio, hoping to get a weather report, but there was little to no signal. Every station was filled with static, and when she gave up, it hit her that the snow might not be stopping any time soon. What if it got worse? What if she was stuck here indefinitely? What if she was stranded in the high country of Montana in a blizzard? Her gas wouldn't last forever. One glance at the gauge and she knew that was true. Just under a quarter of a tank.

Her cell phone. She could call for help. She released her seat belt and reached for her purse sitting on top of the reading material about Dr. Parish. She found her phone and flipped it open. Her heart sank when she realized there was no signal.

"Great, just great," she muttered, then hugged herself and stared out the windshield at the blinding storm. What was it the car-rental agent had said when Kate told her she was heading up here? Snow flurries, that was it. Even Kate knew that this beyond flurries.

She sat back at the same time a light came out of nowhere behind her. The glare of high headlights almost blinded her in the rearview mirror as she tried to make out who or what had arrived. The heavy throb of a big engine vibrated in the air, and she shifted, twisting, trying to see something. Was it a snowplow? Maybe a tow truck? Did they cruise around here in bad weather, knowing that someone would get stuck sooner or later? That made sense to her.

But what also made sense was people prowling these roads, looking for stranded motorists. She'd read enough stories about people who thought they were getting help and ended up robbed, beaten or dead, or all of the above. And she was alone. Completely alone. Unable to run. Then she saw someone out there, a large shadow cutting through the glare of the lights. She turned around, and just as she hit the button to lock all the doors, someone knocked on her window.

The shadow. A huge dark shadow was out there. And any relief was gone. She reached for her purse again, fumbled in it and closed her hand around a small cylinder of pepper spray, thankful that she'd thought to move it from her checked luggage to her purse when she left the airport in the rental car.

She held it tightly as she touched the button for the window with her other hand. As soon as the window started down, icy air rushed into the car's interior and she stopped it before it went lower than an inch or two. She squinted into the night, still unable to make out the features of the hulk out there.

Then a deep, rough voice demanded, "Are you alone?"

Chapter Two

Kate gripped the pepper spray so tightly it made her fingers ache. "No, of course not," she said without thinking. "I'm not alone."

She saw movement and the stranger got a lot closer, blocking some of the cold and wind behind him with his bulky body. A light flashed on, blinding her momentarily until it shifted to the seat behind her. "Is someone else in there with you?"

She used her free hand to shade her eyes. "Could you put that light out?" When the light was gone, and she dropped the pepper spray into her lap and grabbed her phone. She held it up so he could see it. "I meant, I was about to call someone." That was it. She was calling someone, and for all he knew, it was a man, a man who knew where she was, a man who could be on his way right then. "I'm going to call—" She grabbed the first name that came to her "—James. I'm calling James to let him know I'm on my way and let him know where I am and what I'm doing," she said as she turned the phone on. "He'll take care of this."

"If you say so," the stranger said, and he was gone.

Kate put the window back up and looked at the phone, a bit unnerved that her hand was less than steady. The throb of the idling truck behind her was still there, but the man wasn't by her car. She looked at the phone, pressed the search button for roadside service, saw it flash on the screen, then pushed the send button, praying the call would go through someway.

When she pressed the phone to her ear, she was startled by a sharp beeping sound. She pulled it back and looked at the phone's *LED* readout. The "no signal" caution flashed in red on the screen. She turned the phone off, uttered a very unladylike expletive and sank back in the seat. "Damn it all," she muttered, wondering if she'd end up a statistic.

The truck. It was still there, the engine rumbling and the reflection of headlights in her rearview mirror shining in her eyes. He hadn't left yet, and maybe she could get his attention before he took off. If he'd been intent on robbing or killing her, he would still be at the window, trying to get her to open the door.

She dropped the phone onto the seat and hit the horn, once, twice, then again for one long, extended blare. In moments he was at her window, knocking on the glass. The pepper spray was in her lap, and she had the doors locked. She opened the window a crack and shivered at the sudden blast of frigid air.

"What's going on?" he asked. "Your James isn't coming?"

She clutched the pepper spray tightly as she stared

at the hulking figure that was beginning to get a bit
of definition. A heavy jacket with a high collar and
what looked like a cowboy hat pulled low for protection.

"There isn't any signal," she admitted reluctantly.

"I would have been surprised if there was out here
in this weather," the man said.

"How far is it to Bliss?"

"That's where you're heading?"

"Just how far is it?"

"Too far for you to make it in this thing," he said.

That feeling of no control when the car head slid
on the road was transferring to no control over anything at the moment. "If the storm lets up a bit, I
could do it, couldn't I?"

"Maybe, if you have chains."

She wouldn't know what to do with chains even
if she had them on the seat beside her. "I don't know
if I have any," she said.

"Pop your trunk," he said as he headed to the rear
of the car.

She found the lever by her seat and waited while
the man checked the trunk. Moments later she heard
it slam shut. Then the stranger was back by the window. "No chains."

She sank back in the seat. "No driving."

"No driving," he echoed.

"Were you going into Bliss?"

"Through it."

"Could you send someone back with chains or
something so I can get going?"

"There's a garage. They might have chains."

"Perfect. I'll just wait here." She reached for the window button, but the man stopped her, gripping the top of the window with one hand.

"Not so fast," he said, and she stared at his bare hand. A very large hand with strong fingers, short nails and weathered skin. And no rings. "You can't just sit here while I go off to get help. That could take a long time, and unless you've got a full tank of gas, it's going to be a long, cold wait."

"Would it take you that long?"

"Who knows on a night like this?"

If he was trying to scare her, he was doing a good job. She had visions of being found when the spring thaw came, clutching the useless phone and frozen solid. "You think it's that bad tonight?"

"You can see it yourself. This car isn't going anywhere." She heard him exhale. "I don't think you have any option but for me to give you a lift. My truck's a four-by-four and can get there. I can drop you at the garage and they can bring you back with chains." He paused. "And you can call your James from there so he'll know you're safe and sound."

Her James? She regretted the spur-of-the-moment lie, but didn't bother to correct it. What she regretted was that she'd put herself in a situation where she had little to no choice about accepting a ride from a stranger. That wasn't in her comfort zone at all, but sitting in this car in the storm, wasn't anywhere near her comfort zone, either. She choose the lesser of two evils.

"Are you coming?" he asked.

She exhaled. "I'm coming," she said, turning the

car off. She dropped the keys in her purse, along with her phone and charger, but kept the pepper spray in her hand. She looked around, saw the files she'd read on the plane and decided to leave them on the passenger seat. She wouldn't be gone that long. Gripping the suede straps of her purse with the same hand that held the spray, she reached for the door. She'd barely clicked the lock up before the man jerked the door open, letting in a blast of cold that almost took her breath away.

She climbed out and the instant she was standing, she knew that her clothes weren't much protection from the cold. The driven snow stung her face, and she ducked her head into the collar of her jacket, but nothing helped against the chill that was robbing her of body heat at an alarming rate.

Hugging the purse to her chest, she turned and the stranger was there. He looked to be a couple of inches over six feet, but she barely caught more than a glimpse of a dark cowboy hat, before she walked toward his truck. That feeling of being out of control came back with shattering force as she headed away from her car and the known, and toward the truck of the stranger and the unknown.

Her feet sank deeply into the drifting snow, her leather boots offering no protection and no traction at all. She moved cautiously toward the headlights and was very aware of the man following her. As she stepped around toward the passenger side of the cab, the snow seemed deeper.

Just then her feet shot out from under her. She went flailing wildly, grasping for anything to stop her fall. Her right hand hit hard metal, sending a stinging pain up into her arm, then she was falling backward, only to be stopped with jarring suddenness. It took her a second to realize that she'd hit a hard body, that arms were going around her and circling her just under her breasts, and keeping her on her feet.

She suddenly felt safe as the stranger pulled her back against him. "Whoa there," he murmured by her ear as if soothing a skittish horse.

Kate felt the heat of his breath on her skin before he released her. The cold was there full force again and she quickly reached for the hood of the truck to steady herself. The throb of the engine vibrated under her hand in the warm, damp metal hood.

"You okay?" the stranger asked from somewhere behind her.

"Sure, fine," she said, and meant it until she realized that both her hands were pressed palms-down on the warm metal—her empty hands. No purse and no pepper spray. "Oh, shoot, my purse and my..." She twisted around and saw the stranger hunkered down in the snow with his back to her. In the bright lights she saw a dark suede jacket pulled taut over broad shoulders and fur at the collar. A huge man.

Her pepper spray was all she had to protect herself. She'd never taken those karate classes she'd promised to take years ago. All she had for self-defense was that little cylinder of spray, and it had flown off into the snow when she fell. She moved toward the man in the snow, frantically looking around in the brilliance of the headlights, but not seeing anything but snow and more snow.

Suddenly the man was standing and saying, "Found it," and turning around to face her. She knew he had her purse in his hand, but all she could do was stare at the man caught in the brilliance of the headlights. The harshness of the glare cut deep shadows at his eyes and mouth, the hat adding its own shadows, but for a second she was certain she was looking at a rough, unkempt version of Dr. Mackenzie Parish.

No Gucci loafers or Armani suits, but the lines and angles of the face were there the way she remembered from the photos. That frozen moment in time on the tape in James's office. The same face, but different. There was roughness there now. Then again, maybe snow caused hallucinations. Maybe she'd been staring at his pictures so much on the flight out here that she was imagining it now.

Was she imagining this huge man was the famous, playboy doctor to the stars? She had to be. Those hands, large hands, blunt fingers. Not the fingers of a surgeon. She blinked into the driving snow, and the man moved. The shadows claimed his features again as he pulled his hat brim lower to hold the driving snow at bay. "Here," he said, coming closer.

Hallucination. It had to be. She took the purse, the chilly dampness of snow all over the suede, and clutched it to her as she turned away from the man. A moment later she was startled by his touching her upper arm to urge her toward the side of the truck. She moved quickly, getting away from the contact, and wondered if she should just go back to her car.

She didn't turn back. Instead, she slogged through

the deepening snow, feeling the coldness go up the legs of her jeans and into the tops of her boots. Finally she got to the passenger side of the large truck, and the man was there, pressing against her back to reach around her, grab the handle and pull the door open.

He didn't have to tell her to get in. She scrambled up and into the high cab of a very old, very used pickup truck. The plastic seats were cracked, the interior showing more metal then upholstery, but the luxurious wave of warmth from the heater was inviting. She slipped onto the seat and the door slammed shut behind her.

She watched through the windshield as the man walked through the beams of light. Dr. Parish? What a joke. She held her purse tightly to her chest. Nothing about the man matched the doctor. Not the clothes, not the ruggedness, not this truck. Parish's last car in L.A. had been a Porsche, and not just any Porsche, but a prototype delivered straight from Germany. This truck had to be twenty years old and worth maybe a thousand dollars.

She turned as the driver's door opened and the man climbed in behind the wheel, then turned and took off his hat. As he dropped it on the seat between them, whatever she'd passed off as a hallucination took on hard reality. She met shadowed eyes under a slash of brows, a strong chin and high cheekbones set in an angular face. Mackenzie Parish? Twenty pounds lighter, appearing older than his pictures, more rugged and weathered, with flecks of gray in hair that was carelessly brushed back without any attempt to style it?

Could she really be sitting next to the man she thought she'd have little to no chance of finding out here? Was this the famous doctor wearing the rough clothes of a stablehand? She tried to reconcile his appearance with the pictures she'd seen, but then the door slammed shut and the light was off before she could do so.

She turned, closing her eyes, but keeping that image in her mind. Almost, she could almost believe it was him. It was the right place, just the wrong circumstances. And far too much of a coincidence that he'd stumble on her in a storm. She exhaled a shaky breath. Far too unbelievable that the "doctor to the stars," in a storm, in some godforsaken area of Montana, had found her.

Her mind raced. If it was him, she had to be very careful and figure this out before she said or did anything that could jeopardize her assignment. He couldn't be a twin. There weren't any relatives. The brother had died. She stared out at the night, instead of at the man a foot away from her. But she was totally aware of everything he did. The shifting on the hard seat, putting the truck in gear, carefully inching to the left and away from her car, which was slowly being covered by the drifting snow.

The logical thing to do was introduce herself. Then he'd introduce himself. Then she'd know. Simple. She braced herself, then turned and looked at him. "I'm Katherine."

He twisted to look over his shoulder and away from her, then they were on the road and the old truck gained traction, along with some speed. The man didn't say a thing. Maybe he hadn't heard her? She cleared her throat and repeated herself. "I'm Katherine, but my friends call me Kate."

His only response was an abrupt question. "What are you doing here?" He looked straight ahead as he spoke.

She blinked at his profile, and it never occurred to her to tell him the truth, that she was here looking for a man who looked remarkably like him. She'd thought about what to say, what her cover would be, and she went with the story she'd thought up on the plane. "I was going to go to Shadow Ridge, and I thought—"

"You're hell and gone from Shadow Ridge," he said. "You're more than a little lost."

She'd been going to say that she was going to Bliss to spend some time alone before heading out to the ski resort. People in a small town wouldn't doubt that someone from the city would want to get away for a bit, to take a breather. But he'd made that part of the lie unnecessary. He thought she was lost. So she'd be lost. "I asked the man at the car rental at the airport for directions." That was the truth, but the directions were for Bliss, not for the ski resort east of here.

"You should get your money back," he muttered.

"I must have taken the wrong turn after I left the airport."

That did make him cast a quick, shadowy glance her way, and for a minute she saw the man in the pictures. The softness of the dash lights hid the deeper lines on his face, the tightness in his mouth and eyes. Soft shadows etched the almost movie-star-handsome features, and in that moment she was stuck hard by the same innate sexiness she'd noticed in the freeze frame on the video. In a closed truck cab, that look was more disturbing than she'd imagined it would be. She'd found Mackenzie Parish, and judging from what she'd seen so far, there was plenty to write about him.

"You didn't even make a turn," he said, the image gone as he looked back to the road.

Her heart was racing. Luck was ninety percent of life, she'd always been told, and she'd just had a stroke of luck. Dumb, stupid luck, but she'd take it any day. "I guess I didn't," she said, trying to think of something to keep him talking so she could ask questions. "You live in Bliss?"

"No."

A single word. Nothing else. Just no. "You aren't from around here?"

"Born and raised."

"But you said you weren't from Bliss."

"I said I didn't live in Bliss."

It shouldn't be this hard to get simple information out of him. All he had to say was "a ranch outside of town." Simple, but she had the feeling that nothing was simple with this man. "Just where do you live?"

"Around."

Damn him. He wasn't just in hiding, he was shut down completely. And that only made her more curious. "Around where?"

"Bliss," he muttered, and shifted gears.

She needed to take a new tack. She felt in her purse, found the phone and cord and pulled them out. "Can I plug my phone into your cigarette lighter to charge it?" May as well be sure it wasn't dead once she did get a signal. Plus it gave her something to do, for a moment.

He waved at her. "Go for it."

She shifted, pulled the lighter out and plugged in the phone. "Thanks," she said, sitting back as she laid the phone by his hat on the seat.

They hadn't been going terribly fast, but now they were almost crawling along the dark, snowy road. She turned from the man and looked ahead. There were lights, faint and almost swallowed up by the snow, but lights to the right and to the left. "Is this Bliss?"

"Main Street," he said.

She could barely make out the surroundings, except for a few neon lights that managed to penetrate the storm and night. The Alibi Diner & Bar was to the right; Lou's Seed & Feed was to the left; then an orange ball that seemed suspended high in the night was to the right. Gas. The truck slowed even more, then swung toward the sign and stopped.

"Carl's garage," he said as he put his hat on and exited the truck, leaving the engine idling.

Kate braced herself, gripped her purse, then opened her door to jump out of the cab. She felt herself sink into almost knee-deep snow and saw the man ahead of her, a dark silhouette against the weak light coming from high, leaded windows in a sprawling building that was almost lost in the night. She hurried after him, then a door opened and more light spilled out. She made her way toward it and stepped into warmth that was heavy with the scent of oil and grease.

The door closed behind her and she was in a room divided by a counter, with auto supplies at the back, hubcaps lining the walls near the ceiling, tires stacked by the door and a potbelly stove in one corner sending off wonderful waves of heat. A man stood behind the counter in greasy gray overalls. He was a pale man, with freckles, thinning reddish hair and bright blue eyes. When he saw the two of them, he grinned.

"Hey, Kenny, what's happening?" the man said.

Kenny? She looked at the man she could've sworn was Dr. Mackenzie Parish.

"Hey, Carl. The lady's car's stuck south of here and needs chains. Compact car, fourteen-inch tires, two-wheel drive."

Carl looked at Kate. "You were out on a night like this in something like that?"

She stuck with the story Parish had given her. "I thought I was going to Shadow Ridge and ended up here."

"Well, you're way off the track for Shadow Ridge."

"Hell and gone from it," she murmured.

"I'd say so. Now you hold on, and I'll check in the storage room for the chains," he said as he stood.

She turned to the man by her, the man she knew was Mac Parish, despite the fact that Carl had called him Kenny. He was taller than she imagined from the pictures, just one more discrepancy in her preconceived ideas about the man. Then again, he'd always been with tall women.

"So, you're Kenny," she said, not speaking until he glanced at her so he couldn't pretend he hadn't heard her.

He shrugged. "To some."

"And to others?"

"Whatever they want to call me," he said, and deliberately turned from her to get closer to the counter. "Carl, I have to get going. I'll see you later," he called out to the man in the back room.

"You do that," the disembodied voice responded.

Then he turned to her, his eyes, a deep, rich hazel. The color she expected. He touched the brim of his hat. "Good luck," he murmured, and would have moved right past her, out into the night and storm to be gone forever, if she hadn't acted instinctively and touched his arm.

The rough material of the heavy coat didn't hide the sudden tensing in him at the contact, and on some level it pleased her. He wasn't as closed and indifferent to her as he was acting. Whatever, she wasn't going to let him just walk out after Fate had dropped him in her lap. "I didn't thank you," she said quickly, staying firmly between him and the door.

"No need," he said, then broke their contact to move around her.

The only thing she could have done to stop him right then was throw herself at the door to block his escape. She didn't think that would be a good idea with this man. Instead, she had to watch him tug his hat lower, pull up the collar of his jacket, then, flashing a glance at her, walk out the door.

"Great, just great," she muttered, considering running after him for something…anything.

"Bolted, didn't he," Carl asked from behind her.

She closed her eyes for a long moment when the headlights of the truck flashed on. He was leaving. She turned to Carl, the only connection she had to Parish now. "He's in a hurry."

Carl shrugged. "I'm surprised he stopped to help you."

She moved closer to the counter. Carl was obviously friends with Parish. He'd know something. "I'm glad he did."

"The Kenny I grew up with would have helped anyone just like his dad did. But he changed after he came back."

"Came back?"

"He left for a while, went to California." Carl shrugged. "And when Kenny came back to that mess..." He exhaled. "That'd change anybody."

That mess? She'd struck gold. "What happened?"

Before she could ask anything else, the door swung open and cold air rushed into the shop. "Talk of the devil," Carl murmured as he looked past her. "That was fast."

Kate turned as the door slammed shut. Parish was there, snow on his Stetson and shoulders. She felt like jumping up and down for joy, but one look at his face, and she knew he wasn't happy at all. But she'd do whatever it took to keep him right here.

Chapter Three

Mac stood in the middle of the room, cold and wet, clutching the cell phone and charging cord that Katherine had left in the truck. He'd almost driven off, but it had fallen on the floor when he'd started out. Now he was back where he didn't want to be. Involved. He worked at not being involved. His life was involved enough to keep him busy without any outside force intruding on it. Something in him felt as if with one slip on his part, this woman could be very involving. He'd make this fast and get out.

It was the first total look he'd had of Katherine, tall and leggy in a blue corduroy jacket, slim-fitting jeans and boots that would probably fall apart in snow, not any sort of protection. He looked up and met her gaze.

That was another thing he'd hadn't seen in the truck. Her eyes. They were the greenest eyes he'd ever seen, thickly lashed, set in a finely boned oval face. There were freckles on the small, straight nose. Just a few. He hadn't noticed them before, either. And her hair, an almost silvery blond, wasn't done in any fancy way, just pulled straight back from her oval face into a single braid that fell down her back.

It had been a long time since he'd noticed a woman. And now wasn't the time to start. He held out the phone to her, and when she didn't step forward to take it, he moved closer to put it in her hand. The heat was there, on the fingers that brushed his, and he jerked, almost dropping the phone. Then she had it and stepped back, stirring the air around him.

Over the grease and hint of gasoline in the shop, he caught a whiff of something that had been there in the truck. A fragrance from somewhere in his past, but he had no memory to pin it on.

"Boy, I'm glad you came back," Carl was saying, and Mac forced his gaze from the woman to the man. "I don't have chains to fit her car. Not one set," Carl said.

All Mac wanted to do was get out of there and go home. "I guess you'll have to order them," he said, then looked at Katherine. "Have a safe trip."

She frowned at him. "Have a safe trip? You... you're the one who told me I can't drive anywhere without chains, so I guess a trip is out, isn't it, safe or otherwise."

For some reason she seemed angry at him, as if he controlled the weather or Carl's chain supply. He should have driven right past her car in the first place. And he wasn't going to argue with her now. "That was just a pleasantry, not a command."

Her frown deepened. "Easy for you to joke about this," she muttered.

When had this shifted to an argument with a

woman he didn't even know? He was leaving. But before he could turn and walk away, Carl was speaking. "Without chains, she's stuck, Kenny. She ain't going farther then right here."

Now Carl was acting as if he should have answers for this. What was he supposed to do? She had someone named James who could work this out for her, and neither Carl nor Katherine needed his input. "Use Carl's phone and call James." The words were too abrupt, too harsh, but he didn't try to soften them. "Let him figure it out for you."

That logic didn't seem to help at all. "What can he do?" She shook her head as she pushed her phone and cord into her purse. "He couldn't get here."

"Maybe he can send a rescue party."

"A rescue party?" Any anger was gone, blotted out by a sudden smile that put light in her green eyes and curved her pale lips upward. "What's he going to send out?" she asked, her voice slightly husky now. "A St. Bernard with a keg of brandy around his neck? I need chains, not brandy."

He could have used a drink right then.

"I can get your chains tomorrow or the next day," Carl said from behind the counter. "Depends on the delivery service. But definitely not tonight."

She shrugged, and the smile was gone. "Oh, my," she breathed. "What a mess. I didn't expect this to happen." The woman changed her emotions with a speed that left Mac slightly off balance. "I don't know what to do," she said, her finely defined eyebrows lifting slightly as she looked at Mac. "I'm at a loss."

She was looking at him as if he had the answer. He hadn't had answers for anyone for a very long time. "You're in a mess," he murmured.

"You'll have to stay around here for tonight," Carl interjected.

Her eyes widened. "Oh, sure, a hotel."

Mac wished it was that simple. "There's no hotel here."

"A motel?" she asked, still sounding hopeful.

"Nope," Carl chimed in.

"The diner?" she asked Mac. "I could stay there if it's open all night?"

"Nothing stays open all night around here," Carl said.

She turned to Carl then, and the air stirred again, bringing that scent with it. Soft and provocative. *You,* that was what it was called. You. He didn't inhale too deeply as she spoke. "You don't have a room with a cot that I could rent for the night?"

"Sorry, miss, I don't even have a real back room. Just shelves and storage for automotive supplies."

"But not chains," she said.

"But not chains," he agreed with a frown.

She looked back at Mac and drew him into the mess again with another smile that exposed a dimple. "Don't you have any ideas?" she asked.

Any idea he had at that moment wouldn't help in this situation at all. Not when it centered on wondering why that James guy didn't have this woman with him in Shadow Ridge in front of a roaring fire. Heat and pleasure. The man was obviously a fool. "No, no, I don't have any ideas," he lied.

"Hey, how about Joanine?" Carl asked.

That drew her attention away from him again, and as he took a deep breath, the perfume tangled with the air that went into his lungs. "Joanine?" she asked.

"She runs a boardinghouse, well, what they call a bed-and-breakfast. I can call and see if she's got a room."

"Good idea," Mac said. "I've got to get going. I'm late as it is."

"You drive carefully, Kenny," Carl said, then reached for the phone.

Katherine touched him the way she had before, and he realized why his nerves were so raw at the moment. A pretty blonde. A needy woman. A touch. A look. This woman was bringing back a past he'd buried. That was enough of a reason to get the hell out of there.

"What?" he asked, not even bothering to be polite about how he pulled his arm away from her touch.

"I've still got a problem," she said, not reacting to his abrupt severing of the contact.

He didn't want to hear about any problems from her. He had enough of his own. "What now?"

"How do I get to her place?"

Carl cut in right then. "Good news, people. Joanine's got space. She's opened up for someone coming around seven, and she figures that a second guest wouldn't be too much trouble."

"Terrific," Katherine said without looking at Carl. "So how do I get there?" she asked Mac again.

"I'll leave it to you and Carl to work out the finer

points,'' he said, glancing at Carl. ''Your truck's a four-by-four, so I think you're all set.''

''Well, I can't leave for at least an hour or so. Dave's not working tonight. Why can't you drop her off on your way?''

Why not indeed? he thought. Anything he could come up with not to take her with him wasn't worth saying out loud. He knew he'd hesitated beyond a polite period to consider Carl's suggestion when he saw color rise in her cheeks, emphasizing the delicate bone structure. ''Forget it,'' she said in a low voice. ''I can't ask you to take me any farther.'' There was no smile now and he missed it. ''I...I can just call a cab.''

''Never has been a cab service in Bliss,'' Carl said.

Mac looked at her, and he knew when he'd been backed into a corner, neatly and tightly. All he had to do was take her to Joanine's, drop her off and keep going. Simple. So why didn't it feel simple? ''I think you're out of options,'' he said, but meant he was out of options too.

''Is that an offer of a ride?'' she asked, the frown shifting to what might have been a hint of that smile again.

''I guess so,'' he murmured.

The smile was back. ''Then I accept.''

He nodded, then headed to the door with a wave to Carl. ''Take care, Carl,'' he said as he reached the door.

''You, too, Kenny,'' Carl replied.

The cold cut into the office like a knife as he

pulled open the door. "I'll call Joanine's when I find the chains," Carl called after them.

"Okay, thanks," Katherine said. Mac could feel her presence behind him as he trudged toward the truck. By the time he got to the passenger door and opened it, she was there.

She reached past him to grip the door frame and pull herself up into the cab, her purse in her other hand. Oddly, he noticed her hand then, oval nails with no polish, and slender, ringless fingers. Then she was inside, and he swung the door shut as the wind all but pulled it out of his hand.

He hurried around the hood closing out the storm as he got in behind the wheel, tossed his hat on the seat by him and started the engine. Warmth filtered into the cab from the heater, and the windshield wipers groaned under the effort of keeping the snow from clumping on the window.

"Can I ask you something?" Katherine said as he inched out onto Main Street.

"Depends," he murmured.

"On what?"

"On what you ask. It's been my experience that when someone says they want to ask something, it's usually none of their business in the first place."

There was a soft laugh that added to the warmth in the cab of the truck. "You're right...ninety-nine percent of the time."

"So, is this that one percent?" he asked, chancing a quick glance at her. She was sitting with her back partially to the door so she was almost facing him. It made him feel uncomfortable to be under anyone's scrutiny, and with her, he felt even more uncomfortable. "Or is it in the ninety-nine percent group?"

"That's a matter of opinion, I think," she said softly.

If this had been any other situation, he would have thought she was coming on to him. That softness in her voice, that sense of being the full focus of her attention. But that was ludicrous. He had no trappings of money and power out here. And he liked that. He liked the old truck and the rough clothes. Not exactly a turn-on. This wasn't a game between them, just a conversation. That was the old Mac trying to sneak back, but this Mac knew better. "Everything is in this life."

"Exactly. So why don't I just ask, then you can decide if you want to answer it?"

That seemed safe enough. "Okay."

"Good. But there's a question I need to ask before I ask the real question."

It *was* a game of some sort. "What are you talking about?"

"First, who am I talking to and driving with and being rescued by? That man, Carl, he called you Kenny. So, is it Kenny? I really need to know before I ask the question."

It wasn't discomfort he was feeling, it was more like confusion. "First of all, that's hardly one question," he muttered, not sure if his name would mean anything anymore to anyone, especially this woman, but he wasn't going to offer it up to see. "For what it's worth, Kenny's fine."

She hesitated, then, "So, your name's Kenny or is that a nickname?"

"Where are the rubber hoses and bright lights?" he asked.

"Oh, come on," she said, her words tinged with soft humor. "I just asked your name. It's polite if someone introduces himself, which I did a long time back, for that other person to respond with, 'And my name is—'"

"Miss Manners?"

"What?"

"That's what your name really is, isn't it?"

She laughed again, and the sound only added to his confusion. "Sorry, no, I'm just polite, and my last name is Ames, Katherine Ames. And your name is…"

He found himself smiling a bit, an easing of the tension that had been a huge part of his life for the past year or so. "Okay. You shamed me. My name's Mackenzie, a name my mother used when I was in trouble as a kid. Kenny is what I got saddled with because my father was named Mackenzie, too. That meant I was young Mac, small Mac. My Dad got big Mac most of the time, but he hated old Mac. It was easier to call me Kenny, then he was just Mac. I've also been called jerk. That's pretty self-explanatory. So the choice is yours."

"Mackenzie," she said softly. "Kenny, Mac, Jerk."

"Those are the choices."

"What's your middle name?

She never stopped. "Ashton, and before you ask,

that was my mother's maiden name and her name was Ruth.''

"Hmm," she said. "I guess you wouldn't go by your initials, then, would you?"

"What?"

"You know how people get called B.J. or J.R.?"

The easing grew in him as he manuvered on the snow-choked road. "No initials."

"Is your father still alive?"

"No, and what does that have to do with anything?"

"I was just asking, because if he was still around, calling you Mac would be confusing. You said so yourself."

"He's dead, but even if he wasn't, he wouldn't be at Joanine's, so there wouldn't be any confusion."

"Good point," she said. "Okay, Mackenzie Ashton…"

Her voice trailed off and he could feel her gaze on him. No last name. There was no reason for there to be a last name. She'd be out of the truck in ten minutes, and that would be that. "Oh, just call me Mac."

"Okay, that's settled," she murmured.

Why in hell did he feel relieved to have that settled? "Okay, and with you it's Katherine."

"Fine by me. Although, Katherine sounds pretty formal and I've been called a lot of different things, less formal and maybe you should—"

"Enough," he said, cutting her off. "It's Mac and Katherine for the next ten minutes. Then it's goodbye."

"Now, can I ask you that question, Mac?"

There had been no women around in the past year or so, besides Natty, and maybe he was out of practice. Or maybe he'd never really talked to any woman just to talk. Katherine was for talk. That was all. "Okay, Katherine, what is it?"

"Were you really going to leave me there at Carl's?"

Yes, he was way out of practice. "I was leaving, period. If you hadn't left your phone in the truck, I would be long gone."

"You would have made your escape?"

"Call it what you will, I'd be someplace else."

"I'm sorry for inconveniencing you so much."

Now she was making him feel like a jerk. There was no way she'd know, and no way he'd tell her, that just about anything that kept him away from the ranch since he'd come back to salvage his life felt like an intrusion and an inconvenience. "Forget it. I'm going that way…sort of, so it worked out."

"And it's only going to be for the next ten minutes, anyway," she said, echoing his words from earlier.

He glanced at her and found her staring intently ahead of them now. "Yeah, ten more minutes," he said.

She sighed softly. "I never expected to get stuck in this place."

"Next time you'll bring chains."

"There won't be a next time. No snow, no storms, not again." He sensed her shift, stirring the air and bringing him that scent again. "I've got another question."

"You never stop, do you," he murmured.

"Sorry, I tend to be the curious sort, too."

"I'd say you are," he said, slowing to find the entrance to Joanine's property. It was around here somewhere, but the snow was drifting so heavily that it was almost obliterating the old landmarks. Add to that the total darkness beyond the headlights, and he wasn't certain if he'd passed it or even if he was on the right road.

"Sorry," she said again, but didn't sound all that sorry. "I just wondering why you'd live around here."

That brought some of the tension back. "Why not?"

"Oh, I'm not knocking it. I hate it when someone comes to visit or someone's passing through, and all they do is knock where you live. I didn't mean that. But, well, just look outside. It's like another world."

It was another world from what he was used to. "You get used to it."

"How long does it take?"

He actually felt that smile surfacing again. "A lifetime."

The smile died when she said, "Carl told me you left for a while. I can understand why."

Carl talked too much. "Most of the residents leave now and then. It's called freedom. Some actually come back."

"So you came back. Why?"

Just as the tension returned, Mac spotted the entrance to Joanine's. The heavy stone pillars that marked the end of the drive that led up to the old farmhouse had been refashioned by the drifting snow to look like misshapen snowmen. "Now, that's one of the ninety-nine percent. It's none of your business."

"Well, you're blunt, aren't you."

He slowed more and turned right onto Joanine's property. "Why I'm here is no one's business except mine. I live here. Period. And you talk too much."

He'd meant to stop her in her tracks with a rebuke that he was certain would offend her enough to get to Joanine's and get her out of the truck in silence. But he was wrong again. She was actually agreeing with him. "I do talk too much. I've always been curious and, I'm sorry to say, I always will be. It's sort of a curse, I think. That need to know everything about everything around me. You know, the mysteries of life? And one of those is why anyone who'd escaped to California would come back to a place that gets this cold and this snowy and is this isolated. You don't even have a hotel, for Pete's sake."

Carl had told her far too much. Even that he'd been in California. He was getting her out of the truck just in time. "I won't dispute Bliss's lack of amenities. We don't have time. This is Joanine's, at least it is in about half a mile up her drive."

Before she could respond, there was a sound unlike any other sound he'd heard and it seemed to shatter the night. A falling, cracking, thudding, earth-shaking sound that made him hit the brakes and pray they wouldn't skid into whatever was happening.

Snow was everywhere, but not just falling snow. It was exploding upward, too, only to be driven up and off by the fierce wind.

"What was that?" Katherine gasped as she grabbed his right arm with surprising strength. It startled him, almost as much as whatever had happened outside the truck.

She wasn't just a talker, she was a toucher. The type of person who always seemed to need to make physical contact with people. He'd never been comfortable with that, which was why he shocked himself when he had to stop himself from covering her hand with his and telling her everything was okay. He didn't touch her, and even if he had, he couldn't have reassured her, because he didn't know what in hell had happened.

Instead, he reached for his hat and tugged up his collar. "I don't know what's going on. You stay in here, and I'll go see." He opened the door, ducking against the bitter cold and called, "I'll be right back." Then he got out into the knee-deep drifts by the truck, and lowered his hat to protect his face.

"Stay put," he said above the roar of the wind, then shut the door. He went through the snow, into the line of the headlight beams, his progress slow in the deepening drifts. He got near the end of the illumination, stepped to one side out of the light into the dark, and as his eyes adjusted, he knew they were in real trouble.

KATE STARED HARD in front of her, the windshield wipers barely keeping the snow off the glass and doing little to obliterate the crusty patches of frost forming in the corners. Mac had been there in the light, then he was gone. The dark and storm had swallowed him up.

A sense of total aloneness such as she hadn't felt for years assailed her. As a child she'd felt it, but back then she'd read or written or played make-believe to ignore it. But now reading and writing were out, and making believe that she was at home, snuggled in bed, warm and safe, didn't work. Not when the truck shook from the wind and Mac's place on the bench seat was empty.

So she concentrated on why she was here while she sat forward, staring out into the night, willing Mac to come back. She'd found him. No, he'd found her, but either way, she was on a roll. She couldn't have begun to pull off a meeting like this. In a truck, alone with the man. Talking to him. And she knew, if she had enough time, he'd talk.

He hadn't left her at Carl's. She'd had to work on that, but he'd caved in. It hadn't been easy, and she'd hated pulling out some female tricks, but it had worked. He'd resisted talking, resisted giving her any information, but just before they'd been stopped, he'd started answering her. Sort of. Although she'd almost bit her lip when she'd let California slip. She wasn't supposed to know that, but he hadn't called her on it. She'd be more careful when he came back.

If he came back. She was uneasy watching the storm outside. She was losing precious time with him, too. The ten minutes he'd mentioned were ticking away. Soon he'd be gone. She'd be at Joanine's, and she wouldn't see him again. She knew that without a doubt. Nothing beyond a great catastrophe would keep him from dropping her here and heading away.

She strained to make out anything beyond the storm, but there was no movement that wasn't from the wind and snow. A vaguely panicky feeling was starting to take over that aloneness. Mac should have been back by now. He should be here with her, telling her what was going on. She took off her seat belt and reached for the steering wheel to tug herself across the bench seat until she was behind the wheel.

She knew that part of her ability to get a story was her unwillingness to sit still and wait for things to happen. It was also one of her worst flaws. Getting stranded in the snow was evidence of that. But it had turned out great. Right now, she wanted to make something happen. She hit the horn, its blare cutting through the night. She hit it again. Then waited. Nothing.

It was then her imagination kicked into full gear. What if Mac was out there and couldn't get back? What if he'd fallen and was trapped somehow? Something had happened. Something bad. Should she try to drive farther to find him? Or back out and try to get help? Neither made any sense because she couldn't see anything.

What she could do was get out and look for Mac. She pulled her jacket more tightly around her, flipped up the collar, then opened the door. The cold air made her gasp, and the snow stung her face when she tried to look up. She hunched more deeply into her, grabbed the door frame and stepped down. The snow immediately penetrated her jeans and boots.

Then the wind snatched the door out of her hand, slamming it with a resounding crack. She turned toward the front of the truck, toward the light, trying to shield her eyes with her hand. But the cold made her bare hand ache, so she pushed it into her pocket and squinted into the night.

"Mac?" she called, but her voice was lost in the wind. "Mac?" she yelled again.

Only the howling of the wind answered her. She started forward, but stayed to the side of the light, trying to let her eyes adjust to the darkness beyond the beams. Pushing her chin down into the collar, she concentrated on trying to see Mac's footprints. But all she saw was snow and more snow as she went.

It was then it hit her that Mac might have made the trek to Joanine's. He'd said it was less than half a mile ahead. He could be there now, warm and dry, getting ready to come back to get her. She looked up then, shocked to find that she hadn't been going in a straight line, parallel to the lights. She'd wandered off to the right, putting a good twenty feet between herself and the glow. She turned to go back to the lights, but the snow caught at her feet, tripping her, sending her falling.

But this time there were no strong hands to stop the fall, and she went sideways into cold wetness, which went down her neck, up her sleeves, into her nose and mouth. For a split second she wondered if a person could drown in snow.

She couldn't find anything to hold on to, to push off from, to get back to her feet. The darkness and cold were overwhelming, and she was gasping, flailing, totally off balance. In the middle of the madness, she knew she should have done what Mac had told her. She should have waited. She wished she had. Then she heard something as she hit the icy ground with her hand. The horn? Yes! She screamed, "Mac! Mac!"

Chapter Four

Mac found the problem—an ancient pine, more than twenty feet tall, weighted by the snow. It had snapped and fallen right across the road to Joanine's. He went farther, past the tree, checking things out, and finally decided that he and Katherine could walk to Joanine's. Once he got her there safely, he could go back to where he belonged.

As he began to retrace his steps to the truck, he heard something, and even over the wind, he recognized the blare of the truck's horn. Then it came again. He knew that Katherine had to be getting antsy. She wasn't born and bred to this life. This sort of weather did strange things to people, even those who were used to it.

When at last he reached the truck and opened the door, he found the cab empty. She hadn't just panicked, she'd left the truck. He should have made his orders clearer, made her promise not to move. But she'd left in that flimsy jacket and designer boots, regardless of what he'd said.

"Damn it all," he muttered as he turned to look around him, into the night and storm. "Katherine!"

he shouted into the wind. He cupped his hand at his mouth and tried again. "Katherine!"

He reached back into the cab and hit the horn, holding it down for a couple of seconds before letting up to listen. At first he thought there was nothing, then he heard a voice. He wasn't sure if he'd just imagined it until he heard it again.

"Mac!"

He took off in the direction of the sound, stumbling through the snow, but going as fast as he could. There was darkness all around, then he thought he saw something. A shadow in the swirling snow, crazy movement, thrashings, then Katherine crying, "Mac!"

He headed for her, his progress slow, then he was there. He grabbed her hand, pulling and tugging, lifting her, then grasped both her hands. And without thinking he pulled her to him, and the next instant, her arms went around him, hugging him tightly, her face buried in his chest.

The instant he held her, he felt something in him that he'd been trying to keep at bay. He'd known her an hour, tops, and his heart ached from a fear that came from knowing what could have happened to her. That fear caught at his middle and made his hold on her tighten for a moment. God, he'd never been good at being a Boy Scout, doing good deeds. Especially with a woman with green eyes who was threatening to make his carefully constructed new life show signs of weakness in its foundations.

Fear. Real fear. It was harsh, and unwelcome. "What in hell were you thinking?" he demanded with more roughness than he intended. "I told you to stay put. That I'd be back."

"Looking for…you," she said in a voice so unsteady and low that he almost couldn't make out her words.

He held her away from him and saw her chin trembling. "You're a fool," he ground out.

"Oh, Mac," she gasped. "I thought…" She shuddered violently. "I never meant…"

The more he felt her unsteadiness, the more he wanted to get out of there. He wanted her gone. He wanted to be the way he'd been for more than a year—alone. "We need to get back to the truck." He tried to let go of her, but the minute he did, he felt her fade to one side, as if her legs wouldn't hold her. So he had no choice but to keep that contact. He slipped his arm around her shoulder, letting her lean against him, and turned her toward the truck lights.

The snow wasn't letting up, and the wind only seemed to be growing in intensity as he pulled her to his side. She partially hid her face in his jacket, and the going was agonizingly slow. She seemed to have no strength, and the drifts felt like mud around his legs. By the time they got to the truck, Katherine was barely able to walk. He weight was heavy against his side.

Mac pulled the door open, then turned and lifted her into the cab. He pulled himself up and inside, closing the door behind him.

Katherine was hugging herself, her hair partly loosened from the braid to cling to her face. Her jacket was heavy with snow. Where wind should have put high color in her cheeks, she was deathly pale. Her breathing was unsteady and shallow, and she was shaking all over. Mac knew the signs of hypothermia and he also knew that walking to Joanine's was no longer an option. Katherine couldn't go back out in the cold.

"T-Turn up the h-h-heater," she said, her teeth chattering.

Heat could do more damage than good to her right then. She needed to regulate her own body heat. That meant getting her out of her wet coat and into something dry. The only dry cloth was the inside of his own jacket. "Take off your coat," he said.

Her hands were shaking so badly she couldn't begin to manipulate the buttons. He took over, got it undone, stripped it off and tossed it on the floor. Then he tossed his Stetson on the dash, twisted in the seat and tugged off his jacket. Quickly he wrapped it around her, not even bothering to put her arms through the sleeves. "Oh…no," she protested. "Just…the heater…higher," she managed to say.

"No way." He tugged the jacket around her, letting it all but swallow her, and did up the front buttons. "Full heat will only hurt you more." He hesitated, looking at her and fighting an incredibly urge to touch her pale cheek. "Believe me, getting a full blast of hot air is painful when you're this cold. Keep the jacket on." She was about to argue again, but he cut her off. "Just do what I say this time. Okay?"

She stilled and sank back in the seat, the fight going out of her completely. "You disappeared," she said, and shivered violently. "You...you were just gone."

"I told you I was going to see what happened."

"What...did?"

"The weight of the snow toppled a pine tree farther down the way, and it blocked everything. I thought we could walk up to Joanine's, but we can't now with you in this condition."

"J-just give me a minute to get warm."

"It's over half a mile, and you can't possibly make it. Plus, I can't make it without my jacket." He exhaled, wondering why, with his jacket on and the snow making everything damp, he could still catch hints of that damn perfume in the air.

"Then what?"

He turned in the seat. "I don't know. I've got to figure this one out."

Her shaking was beginning to ease, and it showed in her voice when she spoke again. "Well, you're from around here, and I'm sure you're from hardy stock. What does a mountain man do when he gets stuck like this?"

"Beats me."

"Then I guess we'll die."

He looked at her again, shaken when he found her looking wet and forlorn, yet smiling weakly at him. "That's not part of the plan," he said.

"Oh, you have a plan?"

If he did, it wouldn't be to sit in a truck with a beautiful, intriguing woman. "My plan is, since we can't go forward, we'll go backward."

"That's it? That's your plan?"

He gripped the steering wheel and put the car in reverse. "That's it, unless you have a better plan."

"Nope, so I guess we go back. But one question?"

"Another question?"

"About the plan."

"Okay," he said, waiting. "What?"

"What happens then? We go to Carl's?"

"Not an option. It's too far."

"Then what are the options?"

He looked at her again, the glow from the dash lights casting deep shadows at her eyes and throat. "Option, singular."

"Which is?"

He looked away from her focused on his side view mirrors. If he was careful, he could inch back to the main road, and when he got there, he didn't have a choice about where they'd go. He wished he did, but he didn't.

"Well, what is it?" she asked as the truck started to back up slowly.

He didn't look at her. "The only place I know we can get to—with a bit of luck."

He could feel her staring hard at him as he kept his eye on the mirror. "What place?" she asked.

"My place."

Kate couldn't believe it. When the snowstorm had halted the progress of her rental car, she'd faced the fact that she might never make contact with the doctor. And now he was taking her to his house! It couldn't be this easy. Get stuck in the snow, and get your target to find you and take you home? "Your place? Where is it?'' she asked, the persistent shivering still in her voice.

''Down the road a few miles.'' She stared at him as he continued backing down the drive. ''There are no other options or I wouldn't be doing it.''

She was hugging herself under the heavy coat. ''Your place. You and me.''

''Listen, you don't have to worry,'' he said as he stopped the truck as they reached the main road and looked at her. ''I'm not a serial killer.''

What she'd said from stunning pleasure, he'd read as hesitation in going off with him. That worked. It made sense. As far as Mac knew, he was a total stranger to her. ''So you say. But I don't know you.''

''No, you don't, but I do happen to have a place close by, and we need shelter.'' He hesitated before putting the truck in gear and straightening out on the quickly disappearing road ahead of them. ''If it helps, we won't be alone out there.''

''Who's there? Your wife?'' she asked.

''No.''

The housekeeper? The kid? Or maybe he had someone else. A live-in cutey? She wouldn't be surprised. It would be the perfect way to pass a miserable winter, and she felt certain that a man like Mac didn't stay alone for very long. Not after the string of blondes he'd had in Los Angeles. It was a very good story point, and she wondered why it seemed suddenly so distasteful to her.

She barely controlled a shiver and pressed her chin into the soft lamb's-wool collar of his jacket. It held the essence of the man, that mingling of the outdoors and night and something else. A lingering heat. No, that was from the heater in the old truck. Not in the coat. No matter how comforting it had been from the moment he'd insisted she put it on.

"Okay, if you can get your hand into the left pocket of my jacket, you'll find your first line of protection," he said without looking at her.

"What are you talking about?"

"Look in the pocket."

"You pinned my arms in this jacket, so how do I get to the pocket?"

"Use your ingenuity," he said.

"Easy for you to say," she muttered, and twisted her arm inside the jacket, finally managing to get her hand through the sleeve and out. Then she reached in the pocket and felt something there, something smooth and metallic. She pulled it out and in the dash light, she saw it was her canister of pepper spray.

She curled her fingers around it as she looked back at Mac. "Where did you...?"

"I picked it up from where you dropped it back at the rental car. Then I spotted your purse and put that in my pocket." He flashed her a smile. In that instant, the full impact of the sensuality she'd seen in the old magazine pictures was there full force. An almost boyish grin, an expression that jarred her on a level she couldn't explain. "So you're armed now, and safe."

Safe? That was something she wasn't so sure of anymore. "Okay," she said, gripping the cylinder tightly in her cold hand. "I'm armed."

Mac nodded and continued down the road. Kate

shifted and settled back in the seat, and again he got a whiff of that damn perfume. Then it was gone completely. Just gone. Even so, the memories of images he thought he'd left behind were also there. Parties, people, living too close to the edge. "Damn," he murmured, a bit taken back to find the past crowding in on him now.

"Excuse me?" Kate asked.

"Excuse what?" he asked.

"You said damn, and I thought we were in more trouble."

He hadn't been aware of saying anything, and he didn't take the chance of looking at her. He kept his eyes on the road, visible only by the indentation in the snow that it formed ahead of them. "It's just frustrating to have this storm come on so suddenly," he murmured, pushing away his past. "Damn storm," he muttered as the wind hit the truck, almost forcing it onto the shoulder of the road.

"How far is your place?" she asked.

"A few miles," he said.

"Okay, questions?"

"I thought we had everything settled."

"I'm going off with you, and all you've told me is they used to call you Kenny when you were a kid and that we're going to your place, wherever that is. I just want a few answers, that's all."

"Okay, that's fair."

"There, see, you're a fair person. That makes me feel a bit better."

God, if he could have laughed at that moment, he would have. But there was such an edge in him right then, that the humor barely touched the corners of his mouth. "Is that enough for you—that I'm fair?"

"Of course not."

The smile grew a bit. "I didn't think so."

"This place we're going to, what is it?"

"A ranch."

"What kind of ranch?"

"A working ranch—it supports itself."

"Is that hard work?"

"Yes, it is."

"And you came back to Bliss to work on the ranch?"

His stomach tightened and the smile was long gone. "I came back to live here."

"The move's permanent?"

"That's—"

"—none of my business, right?"

"You've got it."

"Okay, then just tell me—"

"No."

"But I—"

"No." His hands gripped the steering wheel so tightly they ached. "Let's keep this simple. You can ask whatever you want. I understand you need to know where you're going, but anything personal is off-limits. Agreed?"

Mac fully expected Katherine to be offended or angry, but she was neither. She simply said, "Whatever," and in some way that annoyed him more then her prying.

"That's the most unresponsive response," he muttered.

"Well, if you'd let me finish my question, you would have found out it wasn't personal," she said evenly, and he suddenly felt as if she'd put him on the defensive. He didn't know how, but she had.

"Okay, what's the question?" he said, wondering how she'd gotten him to ask her for more questions.

"I just wanted to ask how in the heck you know where we are. I can't see a thing in this storm."

That was easy. "Instinct."

"From years of driving this road in storms like this?"

"Whatever."

She laughed again, obviously not a woman who pouted or whose feelings got hurt easily. And he was beginning to like that, despite her annoying curiosity. "Very unresponsive response."

"Sorry."

"Sure you are," she murmured. "So, all things being equal, when do we get to your ranch? I could use a hot shower."

He never took anyone to the ranch, let alone a woman who wanted to take a hot shower. She shivered and he wished that they could go faster than this nerve-racking crawl. "No telling," he said, then asked his own questions to ward off any more of hers. "So, what were you doing out on a night like this?"

There was a hesitation before she said, "Getting lost."

"Oh, the unresponsive response?"

"I was trying to get to Shadow Ridge, and I got lost."

"So this James is waiting for you in Shadow Ridge?"

"James? Oh, James. Yes, he's waiting for me."

That was it. No other explanation. "So you're going to Shadow Ridge because…"

"I need a vacation."

"And you and James were going there, but he isn't with you because…?"

"If you want to know something, don't do that," she said.

"Do what?"

"Do what my high-school history teacher used to do."

He couldn't remember being around a woman who kept him jumping, trying to figure out where the conversation was going. At least it kept him alert. "What does your high-school teacher have to do with anything?"

"Her name was Miss Lincoln, and she'd get up in front of the class and pick one of the students. She'd make you stand, then she'd say, 'Katherine, Attila the Hun was…?' Then there'd be a big pause after her voice went up, and you'd know she was waiting for you to fill in the blank. She couldn't just ask who was Attila the Hun."

"I do that?"

"Yes."

"So you're the expert on question asking?"

"I get to the point. At least, I usually do. Sometimes I get sidetracked when the person I'm talking to won't answer me, but most of the time I don't. I guess I'm pretty curious."

"You? Curious? No."

"Oh, yes, and when I asked you your name, I did just what you did. I said my name, then ended with 'And you're...?'" He heard her sigh. "I never do that. At least not very often, and I don't know why I didn't just say, 'what's your name?'"

"I see your point.

"So, what is it?"

"It's your point," he said, spotting the marker that showed they were near the corner of his property.

"Not my point. Your full name."

"Been there, done that. I thought we agreed on Mac."

"No, I said I'm Katherine Ames, and you finally said to call you Mac, but you never said what your full name is."

She had a way of turning everything around to be about him, and it was starting to wear a bit thin. "We're almost there."

"Where?"

It was as if she'd forgotten where they were going completely. "My ranch."

"Oh, sure, yes."

The wind shook the truck again, and he could literally feel it thwarting their progress, slowing them even more. He saw the buried fences, just humps in the drifting snow, then the bridge made of river stone that spanned seasonal stream, which was usually wide and inviting, but now was little more than a shallow indentation in the snow.

He felt the truck catch traction as he turned onto his land. That brought back memories of when he'd driven onto the bridge more than a year ago. He'd been gone for ten years but was back, looking for the real Mackenzie Parish. He still wasn't sure that he'd found anything but land and hard work when he crossed the bridge, or that he'd ever stopped feeling like the prodigal son.

Sheltered by old oak trees, the drive that wound its way to the house, then beyond to the stables and barns, wasn't as buried in snow as the landscape around it. But it was still hard going. He drove slowly, passing the narrow turnoff to the north pastures, at last spotting the vague outline of the house. Home. His home though even after thirty-five years, it still didn't feel like it.

"So what is it?" Katherine asked.

"Katherine, you can't do that."

"Do what?"

"You started in the middle of a thought."

"No, you stopped in the middle of a thought."

"I bet when you were a kid, you got distracted easily, didn't you."

"And I bet you were annoyingly tight-lipped when you were a kid," she countered without missing a beat.

His childhood was not a place he wanted to go. Michael was there, and the pain was too much. Day-to-day living was enough of a challenge to him now. "You're so distracting," he said without thinking, but as soon as the words were out, he knew the bare truth in them. She'd been distracting him from the beginning and she hadn't stopped. No, distracting wasn't quite the right word, but he wasn't going to look for a better word right then.

"Lights!" she said excitedly, like a kid on Christmas morning. She slapped his arm with the hand still holding the pepper spray. "Oh, look, lights!"

She was a toucher. He looked down at her hand. She didn't even think about touching. Odd that the impulse to reach for that hand was there again, but not to reassure her this time. He realized he just wanted that contact. And that was totally foreign to him. And disturbing. Maybe that was the word he'd been looking for.

But he didn't touch her. Instead, he looked ahead at the glow penetrating the stormy night. "We made it," he murmured, and pulled up in front of the steps to the wraparound porch.

"You did it," she said. "Terrific!" He had the impression that if her other hand hadn't still been trapped in his jacket, she would be clapping.

He left the truck idling and said, "I'll get you inside, then put this away."

"Sounds like a plan," she said softly, and he didn't look at her again. Instead, he put on his hat and exited the truck, stepping into knee-deep snow. The bitter cold cut through his flannel shirt.

The door to the house opened, letting light spill out, and he looked up to see Natty in the open doorway. "Mackenzie, is that you?" she hollered.

"Yes!"

He rounded the front of the truck and heard her yell back, "I was getting worried. You get in here and out of that mess!"

''Keep the door open. We're coming in.''

''We?'' she called back, but by then he was at the passenger door, which Katherine had already opened.

She'd managed to get her other arm through the sleeve and grip the door frame with her right hand. The cab light was behind her, making a halo of her pale hair, and for an instant he felt his breath catch in his throat. Before he could reach to help her, she slid down the side of the truck into the snow, facing him.

''Come on,'' he said, and held out his hand to her.

She looked up at him, and it was then that he realized something was very wrong. She shivered violently, her whole body shaking, then her hand went out toward him. The pepper spray cylinder fell into the snow, and as he reached for her hand, he saw her falling toward him. He caught her and then scooped her up in his arms.

She was completely limp, and he knew that she was unconscious. He turned, saw Natty still in the doorway and called, ''Get the downstairs bed ready. Hurry!''

Chapter Five

Kate was being touched. She felt a hand on her forehead, a gentle contact, warm and careful, and a deep voice was there, more a drone and few actual words. Something about "warming" and "drying," but it made no sense to her. All that made sense was a feeling of safety and softness. Snuggling into that feeling. Relishing it. Not wanting it to stop.

Sleeping? Dreaming? She didn't know until that soft warmth started to dissolve. A chill, then heat again, a cooling, then more heat, the touch, more cold then heat and the comfort was gone. She felt a pain. Something on the surface, her skin on fire, an aching all over, and she heard soft moans that seemed disassociated from reality. Her reality was the heat and cold, the pain and burning and the bone-deep aches.

Then the shaking started, convulsive shivering. Whatever good there had been in the world was gone, except for the voice. It was still there. Deep and urgent, then soft and soothing. Something against her lips, cool liquid that she choked on at first, then managed to get down her throat. The shaking grew until someone gathered her in strong arms, holding her tightly, as if the hold could keep her steady.

And gradually, it did. The shivering lessened, and she snuggled into the warmth, letting that voice echo around her and through her. The voice, saying she'd be okay, that she was fine and safe. That she could sleep now. "Just relax, relax. Rest," the voice said near her ear. "That's it, just relax." She could relax. She could rest. And very slowly, she fell asleep, still being held, warm and safe.

Kate didn't know anything again until she felt herself waking from a deep, dreamless sleep. But it wasn't exactly waking. It was being there, but too weary to open her eyes or speak. She just...existed until she heard voices.

"I wish we could get her to the hospital," a woman said.

"Even if we could, she can't go back outside," a man said.

"I know. I just hope she'll be okay."

"She's doing better." The man's voice was low, almost a whisper.

"What a night. First Tyler terrorizing Mr. Boo to the point that the poor thing got tangled in the light and smashed it, then you show up with a strange woman in tow, an unconscious woman at that."

Tyler? Mr. Boo? This was ridiculous. She wasn't hearing anything that made sense.

"I told you, I didn't have a choice."

"She's lucky you knew what to do," the woman said.

Yes, she was. Kate knew she was very lucky. She didn't know why, but thought that luck had been good to her. More nonsense, she thought, not trying to figure it out.

"We still need to try to contact the man you said she mentioned, that James," the woman said. "Or she has to have family. Someone must be worried sick about her."

Her family? They wanted to contact them in Borneo? That made even less sense to her.

"Or maybe we could call the lodges at Shadow Ridge and ask about her. She had to have made a reservation there."

"Maybe." Someone touched her wrist, holding it lightly, then the touch was gone. "Her pulse is strong, a bit fast, but strong enough, and she's breathing well. Her body temperature is about normal and her color's better."

"You did a good job," the woman said. "But we have to find out what we can about her."

"Okay, but all she has with her is a purse."

"That's a start," the woman said as blankets were tugged higher on Kate.

A hand touched Kate again, this time on the forehead. The man was closer now, whispering to her. "You're okay, Katherine," he said. "Just rest."

Katherine? Nobody called her that. Kate. She was Kate and she'd tell him that…later. But right now all she wanted to do was sleep and stop trying to listen to the other people in the room, stop trying to figure out what was happening.

She let go, and in that instant before she tumbled

back into the comfort of sleep, something struck her. James? Her purse? No, that wasn't a good thing. She didn't know why, but it was definitely not a good thing. Then, it didn't matter.

MAC WATCHED Katherine settle, and something in him eased. Now he believed what he'd told Natty about her being okay. He took a deep breath and for the first time since he'd carried her into the house more than six hours ago, he could actually breathe without tightness. He looked down at her, her hair freed from the braid, the covers up over her shoulders, and her lashes fanned against her pale skin. She'd be okay.

Natty touched him on the arm. "Her purse?"

He looked at his housekeeper, a tall, thin woman who had to be about sixty by now, her gray hair cut shorter than his, her attire the usual jeans and sweater. Natty had been there ever since he could remember, and she had been there when he'd come home. No recriminations, and although she had suggestions, she never really asked any questions. Not like Katherine. "Her purse is in the truck," he said.

"I don't suppose she brought any luggage with her, did she?"

"Just her purse," he said. "We both thought I was just taking her to Carl's to get her on her way." He glanced back at Katherine, who seemed incredibly peaceful now after all she'd gone through. "I'll grab the purse and see if I can get the truck down to the barn."

"Just get the purse. Leave the truck," she said.

"It's sat out in worse. Take care of it when the storm stops." Natty was eminently practical, too. "We need to make a call for her."

The housekeeper was right, someone would be worried sick. *He'd* been worried sick about her and he barely knew her. "I'll be back."

He headed out to the truck and picked up her purse from the front seat. As he turned, keeping his head down against the driving snow, he saw the pepper-spray canister caught in the branches of the barren bush near the walkway. He reached for it, pushed it into his jacket pocket, then hurried back inside.

He met Natty in the hallway coming out of Katherine's room. "She's resting, so let's go and have some coffee and figure this out."

He fought the urge to check on Katherine one more time and, instead, followed Natty into the kitchen, a room that filled the whole back section of the rambling ranch house. She flipped on the lights, flooding the room in a warm glow that spilled over plank floors, stone-and-wood walls, and the sturdy wooden table and chairs in the middle of the space. She crossed to the massive stove, turned the flame on under the coffeepot, then went over to Mac as he took a seat at the table.

He turned the purse over and let the contents spill onto the table—makeup, a hairbrush, a ring of keys, several pens, a small pad of paper, an airline folder, a thin blue book about the size of a deck of playing cards and the cell phone and cord. And a leather wallet. Natty reached for it opened it and read out loud.

''Katherine Marie Ames. Looks like she's from Los Angeles, twenty-seven years old, born on the Fourth of July, five foot ten and 128 pounds.'' She squinted at the wallet. ''Nice picture,'' she said, and held a driver's license out to Mac.

Katherine's solemn face looking back at him. Even in her driver's-license photo, she was endearing. He took the wallet and flipped through it. He found no other pictures at all, just four credit cards and about two hundred dollars in the bill compartment.

''Blast it,'' Natty muttered, and he turned to find her with the blue book open in front of her.

''What is it?''

''An address book.'' She flipped page after page. ''But it's not going to help us any. There're numbers in here, but no names, just initials.'' She read, '''F & I' Looks like a New York area code. There's a J with a Los Angeles area code.'' She turned more pages. ''All the same.'' She looked at Mac. ''What now?''

''She talked about James. Maybe the J is the guy?''

''Could be. So what do we do? Just start calling and ask whoever answers who they are and how they know the girl?''

He looked at the clock on the wall by the windows. ''It's past midnight in Los Angeles and not even dawn in New York.''

''Calling the lodges at this hour makes no sense, either,'' Natty said as she got up and headed for the stove. ''Coffee?''

''Sounds good,'' he replied.

She poured two mugs, then returned with them before she spoke again. "I vote for calling the numbers in her book when it's a decent hour. What's your vote?"

Natty was being sensible. He wasn't. The last thing he wanted to do was call James and say, "I have Katherine here, and because you let her take off alone, she almost died." No, he wouldn't do that. "You call whomever you want to call whenever you want to call them." He put the things back in the purse and reached for his coffee. "I'm going to check on her, then take a shower."

"Just don't wake the baby."

He'd honestly forgotten about Tyler. The boy had been asleep when they'd arrived here and hadn't stirred since. "I won't," he said, and took his mug with him to head back to his room and then to the shower. He passed the bedroom door and kept going, thinking that he'd been right to let Natty call James. He'd never met the man, probably never would, and he felt more anger toward him than he'd felt for anyone for quite a while. Letting her drive off alone in the storm, just letting her go. "What an idiot," Mac muttered.

KATE AWOKE with a start to darkness barely held at bay by a low light somewhere to her right. She blinked, a panic at not knowing where she was or what had happened choking her for a moment. Then she remembered everything, including the pain, the horrible pain and the shaking and the cold.

She closed her eyes for a moment, expecting that

pain again, but felt little to none. A vague aching in her hands and feet, a dull throbbing behind her eyes, but that was it. She lay very still as she remembered Mac and heading to his ranch. They'd been in the truck, her wearing his jacket, and they'd found his place. He'd come around the truck to her, and as she stepped out into the snow…

That was where her memory stopped. There was nothing. Blackness. Then voices. She was in bed, she knew that, and the air was touched by the sweetness of wood smoke. And she was warm. She opened her eyes slowly, trying to focus. In the dim light she could barely make out the thick beams on the ceiling. The walls were lost in shadow.

She slowly turned her head toward the light source, a small lamp with a chimney on it sitting on the nightstand. But the moment she looked beyond it, she felt her breath catch. Mac was there. He was sitting in a chair about two feet from the bed, his dark eyes on her.

"You," she managed to croak.

He stood, and she could see he was dressed in a heavy flannel shirt, jeans that molded to strong legs, and his hair was slicked back from his face. "You're awake," he said softly as he moved toward the bed. "How do you feel?" He was bending over her, then his hand touched her forehead and she had a flashing memory of a hand touching her earlier, softly, and she'd trembled.

"Good, no fever," he murmured, and the touch was gone. "Any pain?"

She shifted slightly, testing her body, and that was

when she felt the blankets on her, flannel, very soft flannel, and directly over her bare skin. When Mac reached for her hand, she evaded the contact and grabbed the top hem of the blanket, lifting it enough to see that she was all but naked under it. She pulled the blanket up to her chin and glared up at Mac. "What did you do to me?"

"Questions again?" Mac reached for her wrist and circled it with his fingers. The fact that she tried to get free didn't keep him from touching her. "You must be feeling better," he said with a slight smile as he took her pulse.

This wasn't funny. Not at all. Here she was in her bra and panties, in a bed in his home. She trembled and tugged to get free. "Let me go or I'll—"

"Shh," he said. "Let me concentrate."

She bit her lip and waited, then he finally let her go and stood back. "Now what do you think I did to you or I was doing to you?" he asked.

She kept the blanket up to her chin. "I'm naked."

That brought a smile to his lips that only made her face burn. "It's best to get rid of clothes when there's a chance of hypothermia, especially if they're wet and cold."

"Well, sure, of course, but—"

"You passed out, and you weren't in any condition to undress yourself."

"Well, of course not," she said, thinking that he was probably used to seeing naked women in his practice, if not his personal life. But that didn't make her feel any better. "So, you just…undressed me?"

"No, he didn't, and you stop teasing the poor girl

like that, Mackenzie.'' A woman spoke from behind Mac and as she moved into the room, Kate saw a middle-aged woman with a pleasant smile and a cap of gray hair, dressed in a chambray shirt and jeans.

The woman was beside Mac now, patting his arm. ''I'm Natalie, but you can call me Natty like everyone else around here. And I got you undressed after Mackenzie carried you in from the truck.'' She rested her hand on Mac's shoulder in a maternal manner. ''Mackenzie took care of the rest. Good care, it seems, from the looks of you now.''

Kate felt an immediate liking for this woman. ''Thank you…both,'' she said.

''Well, honey, you looked pretty awful when you got here, but you sure have good color now and the shivering's stopped. I thought you were going to come loose with all the shaking you were doing.''

Kate had another flashing image of someone holding her. Cradling her. She kept looking at Natty. ''I…I feel okay now. My clothes, where—''

''They're getting dried. I've got an extra nightgown you can use if you like.''

Mac hadn't moved and hadn't spoken, but he kept watching her. It made Kate uncomfortable thinking he might have been the one holding her when she was shivering. Holding her when she was wearing only a bra and panties. A doctor, she told herself, trying hard not to let on that she knew anything about him at all. ''I'm glad you knew what to do.''

''When Mackenzie was a boy, he was always bringing home wounded animals and birds.'' She smiled at Kate as she moved a bit closer and reached down to touch her forehead. Her hand felt cool, and Kate wondered if it was her touch she remembered. "This is a first, to find him carrying a lovely young lady into the house."

She kept her gaze on Natty and said quite deliberately, "He should have been a doctor, instead of a rancher."

"Oh, Mackenzie is a doctor."

"I'm hungry," Mac said abruptly. "And I'm sure Katherine is, too."

Natty frowned at Mac, then the smile was back for Kate. "I bet you are. You've been out like a light for hours."

Kate assumed she'd been sleeping for a quite while. "How long?" she asked.

Natty checked her watch. "Well, Mackenzie showed up with you around eight or so, and it's eleven now."

A few hours, that was okay. Just a few hours lost. "I slept for two or three hours?"

That made Natty's smile grow wider. "Oh, honey, no. You slept off and on for over twenty-seven hours."

"I've been here for a whole day?"

"Food, Natty, we could both use it," Mac said.

"Oh, yes, sure. I need to check on Tyler, then I'll get you both some food and drinks."

Tyler? Was that the child James had told her about? Before she could think of how to find out, the woman was gone and Mac was standing over her. And the longer he stood there silently, the more uncomfortable she became. "Natty's nice," she finally said.

"She's one of a kind," he murmured.

"She lives here?"

"For now."

"She's a relative?"

"No."

"She's your housekeeper?"

"She's whatever she wants to be," he said, "and you're still asking a hell of a lot of questions."

She hated the way he towered over her. Gripping the blanket tightly, she tried to maneuver herself into a half-sitting position with her back against the headboard. The wood was cold on her bare skin, but she stayed like that. "I told you I'm curious, and when I'm in a strange house with a strange man and a strange woman, call me crazy, but I like to know what's going on." She glanced around. "And I can't see my pepper spray anywhere, either."

That brought an unexpected chuckle from Mac, and in that instant she knew what he must have looked like as a teenager. A gleam in his eyes, a soft curving of his lips and a youthfulness that banished the tension in his face. "You got me there. Natty's an old family friend who's been helping me out all my life." The smile was gone as quickly as it had formed. "She's unique."

"And I've been here since yesterday evening?"

"That you have. We tried to contact someone to let them know where you are, that you're okay, but we couldn't make any contacts."

"What? Who?"

"A couple of numbers in your address book, but they were guesses, because all you have are initials with the numbers. I figured the J had to be James, but all I got was an answering machine."

"James," she breathed. He'd be having a fit waiting for her to check in, probably calling the bed-and-breakfast and going ballistic when he found out she'd never showed up there. And her address book? She scoured her memory to think if there were any magazine contacts in it. Yes, there were, but Mac was right. All she ever put in were initials. An old habit that this time, had been a good thing.

"We couldn't figure out how to call your parents or other family."

"They're in Borneo," she said before she thought. "I...I need to call James."

He frowned, but nodded. "Of course. I can bring in a phone for you."

Before she could reply, the door flew open, hitting the wall with a jarring thud. At first Kate couldn't see what was going on, then there was a squeal and something hit the bed on the fly. There was a blur of blue flannel, the smell of baby powder and a rush of cold air. It was then she saw what was going on or, rather, who.

A little boy, dressed in blue sleepers, was intent on getting to her, but Mac had him. He pulled him into his arms, but the boy fought to get loose. His shock of red hair spiked around a face filled with pure enjoyment and dominated by huge blue eyes, he struggled to get down.

That left her sitting there with the blanket down

around her waist, and she made a grab for it. She would have pulled it back up over her chest if the little boy hadn't reached out right then and caught the hem. She tugged and he tugged, and the next thing she knew, Mac and the boy tumbled down onto the bed. There were squeals and muttered oaths, and in the middle of it all, Kate tried frantically to cover herself.

Mac was by her, the flannel of his shirt against her arms, and for a split second she could have sworn that his beard brushed her shoulder, then Natty called, "What in blazes?"

The next instant, the housekeeper captured the little boy, snatching him out of the fray, leaving Kate in the bed with Mac. He was twisting away from her until he was lying prone across the foot of the bed. She scooted back, taking the blanket with her and pulling it up under her chin while pressing against the headboard. Cold was at her back. Heat was at her front, and Mac was at her feet. He turned over, pushed back, and those hazel eyes met hers for a moment before he shoved back. In one motion he was on his feet again. Natty stood there holding the child, watching with a huge smile on her face.

"Sorry, he got away from me," she said. "He heard you in here, and I'd barely set him down when, wham, he was gone." She looked at Kate. "This is Tyler and he's got his own way of welcoming strangers."

Kate wasn't good at looking at a small child and seeing any resemblance to an adult. And she couldn't see any now between the boy with flame-colored hair and Mac. She stared at the boy, wondering if maybe this little human being was the reason Mac had left his life in L.A. to come back here. "Tyler?" she said, and the boy stopped trying to grab Mac's shirt to look at her. "Are you sure it isn't Tornado?"

"It's probably Terror," Mac said as he tucked in his flannel shirt with sharp thrusts. "He's supposed to be in bed."

Tyler squirmed to get down and Natty put him on the floor, but didn't let go of him until she was sure he wasn't going to start another commotion. "You be a good boy and be nice to the lady, okay?"

Tyler frowned at Natty, then turned his incredibly blue eyes on Kate. He approached her, slowly this time, passing Mac without a glance, then he was at the side of the bed. Mac's child? She tried to see Mac in him, but beyond that intense scrutiny, she couldn't see anything of him there. Certainly not with that bright red hair. "Hi there, Tyler," she said.

He cocked his head to one side, studying her, then turned and thrust his hands up to Mac. "Daddy?"

Mac scooped him up and easily settled him in the crook of one arm. "We'll get out of your way." With that he left, and Kate was alone with Natty.

Daddy? James had been right. Tyler was the man's child.

Chapter Six

Mac's child.

Kate was startled when Natty spoke to her as she crossed to a dresser on the far wall. "The boy's a handful, just like his dad was," she said, and took something out of a drawer.

"He's active," Kate said.

"That he is." Natty turned and shook out an old-fashioned flannel nightgown, a soft cream color with tiny roses all over it and ivory lace at the throat.

"This is your room?" Kate asked. "I don't want to put you out."

"Oh, no, it's not my room. It was Janice's and his, but now..." She shrugged. "No one uses it now."

"Janice's?"

"The baby's mother, God rest her soul." She grimaced as if remembering was painful for her.

Kate should have felt excitement, even satisfaction that she'd found out what others couldn't. Instead she just felt a horrible sadness. "She's dead?"

Natty nodded. "Yes, she is." She took a breath. "But that's over and done and we've got the little one, and Mackenzie is back where he belongs. That's what counts.'' She laid the nightgown on the foot of the bed. ''There's a shower through there,'' she said, motioning to a closed door by the dresser. ''There should be plenty of hot water and there's soap and other things you might need.''

This was more than James had even hoped for. Mac had a child and had come back when the mother died. A real story. She looked at Natty, at the pain still there after telling her about Janice. She didn't know what she was going to do with any of this information. It wasn't as cut-and-dried as she'd thought it would be, or the way it should have been, all about a playboy doctor who got in over his head. A doctor who was running from trouble. That was easy. But Mac's coming back when his wife died to take care of his little boy—she exhaled—wasn't easy at all. It was, however, a huge story.

''The little boy, Tyler, how old is he?''

''He's two years old the day after Christmas.''

She wondered what a woman Mac loved looked like. A woman he had a child with. ''Does he look like his mother?''

''Oh, the spitting image of his mama. The hair, the eyes. But he's got the Parish chin, that set way of holding it when he's mad or upset, and that frown.''

''Janice…they were married?''

Natty colored slightly. ''Of course. Oh, I know that isn't always a requirement these days to have a child, but Janice …yes, they were married. And they had the boy.''

He'd been married. That was almost unbelievable. She felt her stomach knot. And Mac had been out on the West Coast seeing every blonde that crossed his path. She felt sick. Or had they divorced? Separated? "He's a cute boy," was all she could say.

"I think so, but then, I'm his unofficial grandma." She looked at Kate, who was still huddled against the headboard clutching the blanket in front of her, trying to digest what she was hearing. "Do you have children?" Natty asked.

"Oh, no. I don't."

"You sound as if that would be a fate worse than death," Natty said with a smile.

"I...I'm not good with kids. I'm not made to be around them," she said. "There's too much to do, and a child takes up so much time." She felt a touch sicker as she realized she was echoing her mother's words. They sounded horrible said out loud, words she'd accepted all her life.

Natty was more sober now. "I've firmly believed that those who want kids should have them, and those who don't, shouldn't have them. But sometimes a person doesn't have a choice, like Mackenzie. He never wanted kids, but he's all Tyler's got in the world now and so he's here for him." She started for the door and spoke while she went. "What did you tell Mackenzie about Borneo?"

"Excuse me?"

She stopped and looked back at Kate. "I thought I heard you say something about Borneo."

"My parents are in Borneo. At least, they were the last time I heard from them."

"What in heaven's name are they doing there?"

"Designing irrigation systems." Kate shrugged.

"My father's an engineer who does that sort of thing."

"I guess you went all over the world when you were a child, then?"

"No, I didn't. They did. I stayed in Los Angeles mostly."

"Mackenzie was in Los Angeles for a while." She frowned. "Too bad you two didn't meet there."

"Los Angeles is huge, and the chances of meeting someone there are minuscule to none." She didn't bother to add that she and Mac didn't travel in the same circles at all. "I guess meeting anyone anywhere is just plain old luck." It had been for her, or she wouldn't be here now.

"Well, dear, I'm a great believer in fate, rather than luck. Look at you. I hardly think that Mackenzie decided to go and get that part for the bailer right then without there being some reason behind it. I mean, bailing isn't something you do in the dead of winter." She smiled at Kate. "I'd guess you're here for a reason," and with that she slipped out and closed the door behind her.

Natty was right. She was here for a reason and at the moment that reason made her feel less than proud. She got to her feet and grabbed at the headboard for support when the room began to spin. She took several deep breaths and looked around a bit. The walls were a rich green with a trim of roses at the top. More roses framed a large mirror over the dresser, and she could see that the blanket she'd been holding on to for dear life was covered with more roses.

A feminine room. And she couldn't help wondering if Mac and Janice had actually lived here together. If they'd made love in this room. Her stomach lurched, sickness rising in her, and she swallowed hard. Her stomach finally settled, and she let go of the headboard, waited, then when the room stayed in one place, picked up the nightgown and crossed to the door of the en suite.

She opened it and found an old-fashioned bathroom and more roses. There was a claw-footed bathtub, a pedestal sink under an oval mirror with roses in the frame, a shower stall with a rose-patterned curtains on, and a vanity that ran the length of one wall, under windows framed by lace curtains.

She hated using the room and being in the bed. She hated that sense of intruding. But she was here. And she was getting her story. She turned on the shower and dropped the nightgown on the vanity. She caught sight of her image in the mirror over the pedestal sink.

She went closer. Her hair was loose and tangled around her face, a pale face with smudges under her eyes and lips that needed color. Janice had to have been a vibrant woman, with flame-red hair, not washed the way like she was at the moment. That stopped her, comparing herself to a dead woman. She had no idea where it came from. None at all. But she didn't like it.

MAC SETTLED TYLER, then went out into the hallway just as the shower in the downstairs bath started. He kept going, past the door and into the kitchen. Natty was there, a pot of coffee on the stove, and she was taking something out of the toaster. She turned when he came into the room. "Cinnamon toast?"

She thought everything could be cured by cinnamon toast. "No thanks, just some coffee." He looked at the clock, a bit surprised to see that it was getting close to midnight. One day and four hours and so much had happened.

"We need to talk," Natty said.

He sank into a chair at the huge kitchen table and shrugged. "Go ahead, I'm listening."

"Her parents are in Borneo."

She said the word as if it was Mars. "I know."

She brought two coffee cups to the table. "Borneo? Who goes to Borneo?"

"Her parents."

She sat down across from him. "And that James person, she hasn't even asked to call him. I thought he was a boyfriend or something, from what you said and if it were me, I'd be demanding a call."

"She did and I told her I'd get the phone, but Tyler burst in right then and we got sidetracked." He sipped some coffee, then looked at Natty. "Do I need to ask where you're going with this?"

"What if she's running away from something or someone?"

"Like what?"

"The police or someone who's after her for some unknown reason."

"You've been watching those reality TV shows way too much." He fingered his mug. "She's not some serial killer."

"Probably not," Natty said. "But don't you find it odd that she came to Bliss in this weather at this time of year?"

"She was going to Shadow Ridge."

"So you said." She frowned at him. "Are you sure that was where she was trying to go first?"

"Why?"

"She had a paper in her purse, just folded over. It said something like 'Bliss, 7, BB' on it. I thought she was meeting someone with the initials B.B. in Bliss."

He shook his head. "That could mean anything."

She sat back. "Maybe," she said, but didn't sound convinced. "If she's running away, no one's going to find her here, are they?"

"Not in this storm."

"She's really lucky you found her like that. You'd have thought you two would have met in Los Angeles or something."

"Los Angeles is a world unto itself, and just as big. How in hell would we ever have met there?"

"I don't know. I haven't asked you a whole lot of questions, have I. So how would I know?"

"You're good at keeping quiet," he allowed, then took another sip of coffee. He'd just walked into the family home one day and Natty had taken up with him as if he'd never left, as if it were as natural as breathing for him to take over as father for Tyler. "I appreciate that about you."

"I don't pry. I don't tell you how concerned I am about you not sleeping, about you not being around anyone except the boy and me. I've left you pretty much alone, haven't I?''

He sat back, cradling the mug in one hand. "Now where are you going?"

Natty put down her mug and looked right at him. "Okay, word is, Dr. Peters at the clinic is going to retire after the first of the year, and there isn't anyone to take his place, and I was thinking that—"

"Stop right there." He'd never expected this. "I'm no family doctor. I'm no doctor anymore."

"Of course you are. Look what you did for her." She waved her hand in the general direction of the bedroom. "Good grief, you saved her life."

"I did what a Boy Scout with first aid training could have done."

Natty exhaled noisily. "Mackenzie, are you going to leave again?"

"Why would I leave again?"

"I don't know. I just thought that maybe, with her here and all, you'll remember what you used to do out there in California and start missing it."

"What does she have to do with it?"

"She's pretty, blond, a lovely woman. Do you think I didn't keep track of you while you were out there?"

Natty had never brought this up before and it took him by surprise. "You kept track of me?"

"Oh, it wasn't hard, not with all those stories about you popping up in the magazines and newspapers."

He sighed. His past seemed to belong to another

person, not him. "I can't believe you'd read that rubbish."

"It wasn't true that you were dating that moviestar, the tall blonde girl with hair that looks like it's been combed in a blender? I can't remember her name, but I think it was the name of a state, like Alabama or Mississippi or—"

He remembered. "Dallas. A city."

She sat forward. "So you did date her?"

"Once."

"See, that's true. Is the rest of it true?"

"I'm no saint, you know that."

"I never thought you were."

"But I don't think I would have had the stamina to do what they claimed I did." He tried to make a joke of it, but she wasn't having any of that.

"You ran wild out there, and Michael..." She must have seen him flinch, because her voice trailed off before she finished with, "This must all seem so boring to you here. I was glad when you called and said you were coming back, and I really expected you'd only be here long enough to make sure the boy was okay. Then you stayed." She smiled softly at him. "I'm so proud of you for doing that."

Remembering brought pain, which made him speak more abruptly than he meant to. "Stop it." Her face reddened and she sat back as if he'd slapped her. He'd hurt so many people, and now Natty. "I'm sorry," he murmured. "I don't want to talk about this. I'm staying. Isn't that enough for you?"

She nodded, then sipped more coffee before she spoke again. "And when the doctor leaves?"

"Forget that, okay?"

"For now."

That was the best he was going to get out of her, and he knew it. "One other thing, Natty?"

"What?"

"I don't want Katherine to know anything more about me than she already does."

"Why?"

"Because it's none of her business," he muttered.

"Okay, it's none of her business," Natty echoed as she looked past him.

"What's none of my business?" Katherine asked from behind him.

Mac turned toward Katherine while he tried to figure out what to say. But when he saw her, he was silent. She stood in the doorway, her hair damp and loose, combed straight back from her makeup-free face. Freckles brushed her nose, and deep shadows smudged the skin below her green eyes. She wore a long, flannel nightgown that covered her from neck to foot, and he didn't know how she could look so sexy in it. But she did. He quickly turned back to his coffee when she started into the room.

"I didn't want you to know that we went through your purse," he said. Stupid thing to say, but the best answer he could come up with.

"I told Mackenzie that no woman wants a man to read her driver's license." Natty smiled at Katherine. "You need to sit. You look as if you could use a good cup of coffee."

Katherine moved to the table and sat down by Mac

with a sigh. "I'm probably the only person on earth who doesn't drink coffee."

Natty was moving toward the stove now. "How about tea or cocoa?"

"If you have cocoa, I'd love some," she said. "This kind of weather seems perfect for cocoa."

Mac glanced over and saw her press both hands flat on the tabletop. Slender fingers, pale-pink oval nails and no rings. He'd noticed that before, no rings. "You wanted to call James?" he said.

"Oh, yes, I did." He could see her pressing her hands to the table again, as if flexing them some way. "Are your hands aching?" Mac asked.

He met her gaze. Those incredibly green eyes narrowed slightly as she glanced down at her hands. "Yes, a little."

He held his hand out over the table, made a fist, then splayed out his fingers before forming a fist again. "Do this a few times. It should help."

She started doing it, then smiled at him, an expression that startled him. "Shoot, you're right. That feels a lot better. I was sure I'd never be able to type again."

Natty placed a mug in front of Katherine. Marshmallows bobbed in the steaming chocolate, melting slightly from the heat. "Oh, thanks," Katherine said with the delight of a child. "I haven't had cocoa for...forever, it seems, and with marshmallows, too."

Natty sat back down, took a sip of her coffee while Katherine stirred the cocoa with her spoon. "So, you're a secretary?"

The spoon stilled and Katherine looked at Natty with a puzzled expression. "Excuse me?"

"You said you didn't know if you'd be able to type again, and I assumed you were a secretary."

"Oh, no, I'm not," she said, putting down the spoon and taking a small sip of the hot chocolate. "Mmm," she said softly, as she put the mug back on the table. "That is incredible."

She had a small line of chocolate on her upper lip, then her tongue flicked out and it was gone. Mac looked away quickly and got to his feet. "I'll get you the phone," he said over his shoulder as he crossed to the counter and reached for the cordless phone.

He heard Natty behind him. "So, you were heading to Shadow Ridge when Mackenzie found you?"

"Yes, I was."

"You're a skier?"

He gripped the phone and turned to go back to the table as Katherine laughed softly. "Not in this lifetime. I can't stay on my feet on skis."

He held the phone out to her. "What's the point of going to Shadow Ridge at this time of year if you don't ski?" he asked as she took the phone from him. He felt her fingers brush his, and he felt something akin to an electric shock tingle through him. Static electricity? He drew his hand back and sat in the chair again, then reached for his coffee mug.

"I like watching," she murmured before taking another sip of her chocolate. "Being with...friends. I just didn't know I'd get lost in this blizzard." Her cup touched the table with a soft thud, and he saw her shiver slightly. "Or that it would be so horribly cold." To his dismay, her smile was gone completely. "I don't know how you people live through winters like this."

"We're hardy folk up here," Natty said.

"I'd say so," Katherine murmured as she glanced at Mac again, but made no attempt to use the phone. "I'm not the hardy type."

He wasn't going to go into what type she was. He veered back to what Natty had asked her earlier. "So what do you do in L.A.?"

Kate knew that the best way to lie was to tell the truth as much as possible. She told Mac the truth. "I write."

His eyes narrowed and she saw the way he stilled. "You're a writer? What kind of writer?"

"A starving writer," she said, hoping to smooth the way to some other topic.

Natty laughed. "Starving in a garret?"

"No, in an overpriced apartment."

That made the other woman laugh again. "Isn't that all there is in Los Angeles?"

"Seems that way," Kate said.

"So, dear, you write. What sort of writing do you do?"

She gave a bare truth to that question. "Mostly research at the moment."

"And it doesn't pay much?" Natty asked.

"No, it doesn't pay nearly enough," she said truthfully.

"Going to Shadow Ridge isn't cheap," Mac said.

"You're right, but I'm not paying for it."

"James is?"

The truth. "Yup. Everything."

Mac motioned to the phone in her hand. "Aren't you going to call him? He must be going crazy if he expected you last night. You owe him that much."

When they'd dated, James had thought that buying someone dinner meant that you owed them. "I don't owe him anything," she said tightly, "except the courtesy of letting him know where I am."

His eyes narrowed again, and she knew she couldn't let anything personal penetrate this exchange. Mac wasn't stupid, and she didn't want him to read anything into her responses. "Whatever," he muttered.

She hated it that her fingers weren't exactly steady when she dialed James's home phone number. A holdover from the cold, she thought as she put the phone to her ear and heard it ring. She glanced at the clock. It was around midnight in Los Angeles, but James didn't answer the call. His machine picked up. "This is a machine and you know what to do." She'd always disliked that message.

After the beep she said, "Hi, there," not letting on she was on a machine. "I'm sorry, I'm sorry. I got lost when I left the airport and ended up in the middle of this storm in a place called Bliss and I couldn't call until now." She paused as if he was speaking back to her, then without putting her hand over the mouthpiece, she looked at Mac and asked, "Where am I, exactly?"

Natty spoke before Mac could. "You're at the Parish Ranch on old Route 2, number seventy-two on the box.''

She repeated that to James's machine just to make sure he got it, then said, ''Of course, I'll be okay.'' She paused. ''Of course. Of course.'' She looked at Mac. ''Mr. Parish has been a godsend.''

She paused again before saying, ''Okay, me, too.'' Another pause to the empty line, then, ''Of course I do. I'll call you to let you know as soon as I find out. Bye.'' She hung up, then put the phone on the table.

''He's in Shadow Ridge?'' Natty asked.

''He's warm and dry and probably drinking brandies by a fire.'' That part was very true. James and his brandy and a roaring fire. The perfect seduction scene for him. She cringed at how close she'd come to being a casualty of that scenario.

''At least he knows you're okay. He must have been going mad wondering what happened to you,'' Natty said.

''He knows now,'' she said, and sipped more cocoa. She'd always said or done what it took to get a story. That was part of the deal with this job, but at that moment, the lies didn't sit easily with her. She looked out the windows over the sink, at the snow sleeting against the panes. ''Is this ever going to let up?''

''It let up some today, but started again just before you woke up,'' Natty said, and barely covered a yawn. ''I'm going up to check on the boy, then go to bed.'' She looked at Kate. ''I dried your clothes, but if they aren't usable, you might be able to find something to wear in the closet in the morning. Janice wasn't as tall as you, but you're about the same size otherwise.''

The idea of wearing Mac's dead wife's clothes was unsettling, to say the least. She'd been thankful the nightgown was Natty's. ''Thanks,'' she said. ''But I'm sure my clothes will be fine.''

''You get back to bed,'' Natty said. ''You look exhausted.'' Her gaze swung to Mac. ''I know better than to tell you to go to bed,'' she said. ''But try to rest. Oh, there's stew or chili if you two want to eat—just heat it up.'' With that, she left.

There was just a bit of cocoa remaining in her mug, and Kate jiggled it, watching the chocolate swirl. ''I need to say something,'' she began.

''You've already thanked me.''

She glanced at Mac's hands holding his mug. She couldn't get over the size of his hands. One thing she'd always heard about surgeons was that their hands were usually refined with slender fingers. But his hands looked strong and sturdy. ''No, it's not that.'' She made herself look up at him, meeting his gaze, and braced herself. ''I hope you aren't uncomfortable with me in that bedroom.''

''Why would I be?'' he asked.

''I mean, it was…Natty said that it was your room.''

He shook his head. ''You misunderstood Natty. That's not my room.''

''I meant, before. You and your wife had that room?''

He looked taken aback. ''My wife?''

"Natty said that Janice and you were married, and…" She saw the tension in his face, the way the lines at his mouth deepened and his hand tightened on his mug. She'd gone too far, too fast. She tried to ease back. "Never mind," she said quickly. "That's one of those ninety-nine percent things, isn't it."

"Damn straight," he muttered. "Damn straight."

Chapter Seven

Kate met Mac's gaze, and she flinched at the pain she saw there. She hated herself at that moment. "I'm sorry. I shouldn't have said anything about that."

He exhaled roughly, then shook his head. "Forget it," he said, then pushed the coffee mug away from him and stood. "Are you hungry?"

Actually, she was. "I think the last thing I ate was a what-is-it sandwich at the airport."

"Been there, done that," he murmured as he crossed to the refrigerator. "Chili or stew?"

"Either is fine."

He returned with a large bowl in his hand. "Stew it is," he said as he crossed to the big stove. "You could use the protein."

Kate sat back in the chair just watching him. He found a pot in a cupboard by the stove, and within moments the stew was heating. Mac crossed to the sink and ran water over his hands, then, as he dried them on a towel, he stared out the window.

She saw the way he took several deep breaths, the way the action stretched the fabric of the red plaid shirt, then the way he dropped the towel on the counter and pressed both hands to the edge of the sink. He seemed to slump, lowering his head a bit. Then with a harsh intake of air, he straightened up. Kate hardly knew the man, yet she sensed his pain. "You're tired?" she asked.

He sighed and turned to her, his face passive. "Janice wasn't my wife," he said.

All she could do was look at him. "You...you were divorced?"

"No, we were never married," he said.

"Natty said that—"

"You misunderstood."

So they'd lied to Natty, or Natty covered for them? A woman sat here with his child, while he was in L.A. living the good life? She didn't know why that made her feel so damned disappointed in the man. "Oh, I see," she breathed.

"What do you see?" he asked, that tightness flitting at his mouth and eyes again.

She shrugged. "I just meant that you don't have to explain anything to me."

"No, I don't, but just for the record, Janice was married to my brother."

His brother? "But I thought...you and Janice and Tyler..."

"Janice and Michael, my brother, were Tyler's parents."

"He calls you Daddy."

"He's so young, he doesn't remember his mom and dad, and Michael and I looked a lot alike."

"Looked?"

''He's dead,'' Mac said bluntly.

She knew that, but it didn't stop her automatic sympathy at what he'd lost. ''Oh, God, I'm sorry,'' she whispered.

''Sure, everyone is,'' he muttered.

She'd never believed you could feel another person's pain. Not really. Not until that moment. She felt an ache in her that had everything to do with the look in Mac's eyes. ''I shouldn't have asked. I ask questions without thinking sometimes.''

''No apologies needed,'' he murmured. ''Unless you're psychic, how could you know?''

Because she had a thick file on Dr. Mackenzie Parish. She wanted to stop this whole conversation. Just make it go away. And then maybe there would be some easing in Mac. ''Without looking into my crystal ball, I can tell you that the stew's going to burn if you don't stir it or something,'' she said, looking past him at the stove and the steam rising from the pot on the burner.

Without a word he turned, picked up a wooden spoon and stirred the concoction.

It was too hard for her just to sit there at the moment. She needed to move. ''Where are the dishes?''

He motioned to cupboards on the side wall near the refrigerator. ''There, and the silverware is under the counter.''

But when Kate rose to get dishes, the room seemed less than steady and her legs felt weak. She held onto the back of her chair, let everything settle, then crossed to the cupboards. She found two large bowls, some silverware, then crossed to Mac by the stove. "Here," she said, offering him the bowls.

He took them from her and for a long moment, looked down at her. "You're pale," he said. "Sit."

She wasn't going to argue, not when her legs felt like rubber. She went back to the table, sank back down in the chair, then laid out the silverware. By then, Mac was there with the bowls of stew, a box of crackers and the pot of coffee. "Sorry, I didn't think to make more hot chocolate for you," he said as he sat.

She picked up her spoon. "Food is what I really need."

She tasted the meaty mixture and found it delicious. "This is fantastic," she said, reaching for some crackers.

"Natty's a great cook," he said.

They ate in silence, until Kate pushed her almost-empty dish back. "I am so full," she said.

Mac's dish was only half-finished, but he, too, pushed it away, then poured himself more coffee. Sitting back, he sipped the coffee as he met her gaze over the rim of the heavy mug. "I was going to ask you what got you into research writing, but from the way you ask questions, I'd say it's a fitting field for you," he said, startling her with this conversational direction.

The lying had been forgotten for a while, but now it reared its ugly head. She put the spoon in the bowl, then swiped at a few cracker crumbs on the tabletop. "I'm curious and I like finding answers for things, but research isn't what I want to do in the long run. I mean, for now it's a living…sort of.''

"What would you do if you didn't have to make a living?'' he asked.

"Things.''

"Such as?''

Right then she found herself admitting something that had been lost to her for years. A dream that had been pushed away in the rush of her life. "If I didn't have to make a living, I'd write a novel. Fiction, no facts.''

He smiled at her, apparently amused. "The Great American Novel?''

She didn't want that smile from him. She'd seen it before, just before she'd let the dream go. She'd once told her mother what she wanted to do, and been told it was a useless goal that wouldn't change the world. Changing the world had been, and still was, high on her parents' agenda. But she didn't want to be humored by this man or ridiculed by him. "Just a novel, my novel.'' She'd thought that dream was dead, and it was shocking to find it was still alive…barely. And more incredible that she had told Mac about it.

Fortunately he let it drop. He stood, picked up the dishes and took them to the sink. Quickly, he rinsed them, then turned back to Kate as he dried his hands. "How about a glass of wine?''

She didn't want this growing sense of intimacy in the room, a connection that couldn't happen. Not with Mac Parish. "No, thanks.''

He tossed the towel on the counter and leaned

back against the counter edge, crossing his arms on his chest.

She made to stand and head to bed, but the minute she tried, her legs gave out. She reached for the table for support, but Mac was there, catching her by her arm, steadying her, letting her get her balance. "Hey, take it easy."

She hated needing his support again. She wished she could just move away from him and that fragrance of soap and water and a certain maleness would disappear. But she couldn't stand without him at that moment. "My legs are weak."

He was even closer. "Lean on me," he murmured, and had his arm around her, supporting her the way he had that night they'd tried to go to Joanine's.

She closed her eyes tightly, wanting desperately to say she could walk and he could let her go, but that was a lie. "Thanks," she whispered, and let him help her back to the bedroom.

The room felt cool to her, and Natty had obviously been in there—the bed was made and a pale-blue robe was laid out on the rose comforter. She got to the bed and would have reached for the foot post for support, but she was too weak to do even that. "Climb in," he said, tugging back the comforter and sheet and he helping her into bed.

She felt like a child. Or at least how a child would feel being tucked in. She couldn't remember her parents ever being there at bedtime. But she let herself fall into the softness of the bed, lying back on the pillows and sighing with relief. "Thank you," she murmured, and closed her eyes, waiting while the world fell away.

She felt him touch her cheek, and she slipped into the softness with a sigh. But before she could let go completely, she felt his lips brush hers, the mere suggestion of a kiss, and then it was gone. A dream? A wish? She didn't know, and in that moment between sleep and waking, she didn't care.

Even at his worst in Los Angeles, even when he'd taken the easy way out, even when he wondered if he had much of a conscience, Mac never took advantage of a woman. He'd never done anything that irrational, but he was teetering perilously close to violating his carefully constructed rules when he kissed Katherine.

He didn't know where the kiss had come from any more than he knew where the need to get closer to her came from. An intense ache in his being, the solitude that had been his goal for more than a year, seemed hollow and painful at that moment.

What sanity he had came into play and he drew back, giving himself distance to cement that sanity. He'd been alone out here too long, and he was losing it. So he did the most rational thing he could think of. He walked away and didn't look back as he exited the room.

He was out in the hallway, alone, moving farther away from her, and he wondered how in the world he could still taste her on his lips. He headed back into the kitchen, went into the mudroom by the rear entry and found his jacket. Slipping it on, he grabbed his Stetson off the shelf and went out into the stormy night. The wind cut into him, and he ducked his head. He could make out the security lights on the stable and headed through the deep snow toward them.

Sleep wasn't something that came easily to him anymore, so he trudged toward the lights and tried to ignore the ache in his middle. He'd made a project out of not thinking about what he was responsible for. To just live life day to day and do it the best he could. But Katherine's presence and her questions were muddying the waters.

He exhaled and jammed his hands into the pockets of his jacket, finding the pepper-spray canister he'd tucked in there. He closed his hand around it tightly. Later he'd figure things out. Right now, he'd check on the horses. He'd do something, anything, but think about Katherine in the bed. Then he'd sit alone in the den and get through the night.

KATE AWOKE to a morning that was storm-free. Cold, gray light came in through the frosted windows. As she lay there in silence for a moment, she heard tiny feet running by her door. Tyler. Heavier footsteps after him. But not as heavy as last night. Natty.

She pushed herself up and got out of bed to pad barefoot to the window. She looked out at a world of beauty she had never seen before. Waist-deep snow, huge trees all but swallowed up by the weight of the snow, everything covered in white. A new day. She felt stronger now, her legs steady. She touched the frosted windowpane, felt the coldness under her fingertips and suddenly remembered what she thought was a dream.

Climbing into bed. Mac touching her cheek. Mac kissing her? No, that had to have been a dream. Part of whatever had happened to her last night when all her strength drained out of her. If not a dream, a hallucination. Not reality.

She turned, gathered her dry clothes from where Natty had left them, then went into the bathroom.

Fifteen minutes later Kate left her room and headed toward the kitchen and the fragrance of bacon frying.

She stepped into the room and found Mac sitting at the table with Tyler in a booster chair. Toast and jelly were smashed on the tray in front of the boy, and some of the jelly stained his face and overalls. He was making every effort to evade the spoonful of scrambled eggs Mac was trying to feed him. ''Come on, buddy, it's good, really good.''

Kate stood in the doorway and watched. Mac looked as if he hadn't slept well—his eyes were shadowed, and a new beard darkened his jaw. His hair was slicked back damply, and he was wearing jeans and a chambray shirt with the sleeves rolled up and the neck open. He leaned closer to the boy. ''Buddy. Food. Eat.''

The boy looked up and grinned at Kate. Mac turned then, and his eyes flicked over her. There was nothing in his expression that told her if anything had happened last night. He simply nodded to her, murmured, ''Good morning,'' and turned back to the boy. He held the spoon up again. "Come on, buddy, eat."

She could see Mac's frustration and wished she knew something about kids that could help him get Tyler to eat the eggs. But she didn't have a clue how to persuade a child to eat anything. Mac pretended the spoon was a train chugging toward the boy. That didn't work. He pretended the spoon was a plane ready to land. That didn't work, either.

She moved toward the pair, but stopped when Tyler suddenly made a grab for the spoon, catching Mac off guard. Tyler hit the food-laden spoon, sending it into the air, and squealed with glee as egg flew everywhere. Kate watched as the mess fell, part of it in Mac's hair, part on the table and the rest on the floor. The spoon followed suit, heading right for Mac's head. Kate yelled, "Watch out," as the spoon struck Mac in the shoulder, bounced off and onto the table, striking a plate full of bacon.

Mac flicked at the egg in his hair, then brushed at his shirt, sending the yellow particles to the floor. He looked at her, then at the boy and slowly rubbed his hands together as he shook his head. "Admirable coordination, buddy," he said. "But that's it. I'm not wearing any more of your breakfast."

His voice was low, but he didn't seem angry. He wasn't going to shout. He eased himself out of the chair, and then stopped moving. He glanced at her again, and his eyes didn't look right. Was he sick?

Tyler squealed. Mac flinched at the noise, and Kate asked, "Are you okay?"

"I'll survive if he doesn't do that again," he said, then asked, "How are you with kids?"

"Me? Oh, no, you've got the wrong person."

"That's what I used to say," he muttered, easing himself to his feet, then slowly moving away from her and the boy to the counter. He poured himself a cup of coffee, took a careful sip, then turned back to her, cradling the mug in both hands. "How long can it take to change a crib?" referring to Natty's disappearance.

"As long as it takes," Natty said in a cheerful voice from behind Kate, and Mac flinched.

"Good heavens, can you stop shouting?" he ground out.

"I didn't think I was shouting." She crossed directly to Tyler and sat down in the chair Mac had just vacated. She smiled at the boy who was mushing a big piece of toast into the wooden tabletop of. "Egg everywhere, and I don't have to ask who did it," she said.

Tyler looked at Kate, and for an instant, she finally saw Mac in him. That frown, the narrowed eyes, then it was gone as he held out a piece of toast to Natty. "No thanks," she said. "I'll make my own." She picked up the bits of egg on the table, putting them back in the dish as she spoke to Kate. "How are you doing this morning, Kate?"

"Better, thank you."

"You look better, and you definitely are doing better than he is." She motioned with her head to Mac as she continued picking up the mess.

Kate glanced at Mac, but he was staring into his

coffee mug as if its contents were the most important thing in the world. Then Natty said to her, "Sit down and have some toast." She pointed to a plate of toast that appeared untouched. "Help yourself."

Kate took a chair on the other side of the boy, then reached for a slice of toast. She broke it in half and sensed Mac moving behind her. But he didn't come into her range of vision.

"I'll be back," he muttered, and she turned to see him crossing the room to an open door. Before he got there, she spoke up.

"Mac? Do you think Carl has the chains yet?"

He stopped and looked at her, his eyes narrowed as if the sight of her was painful. Maybe the sight of anything was painful for him at that moment. "I called him yesterday and let him know you're here. He didn't have the chains yet. But the storm's not over. They're expecting more snow today."

If she had planned being stranded with her subject, she couldn't have done better. Odd that instead of feeling excitement at having more time to get what she wanted, she felt uncomfortable. "We can't even get back into Bliss?"

He shook his head and stopped midmotion, grimacing, then exhaling. "No. We can't." With that, he left the room.

Moments later she heard a door open. A shaft of cold air rushed into the room, then the door slammed and the cold was cut off. She glanced down at the half-eaten toast in her hand and said, "Where did he go?"

"Stables or barn," Natty said. "Wherever he can get to through the snow. Maybe he's just walking."

Kate looked at the woman who was doing her best to keep Tyler from spitting out a piece of bacon. "Mac doesn't look well."

"He's as well as can be expected," Natty replied, taking the food totally of the boy's reach and leaving him to play with the toast he'd already ruined. "If he could get a good night's sleep, he'd do better," she said.

A thought came to Kate with jarring suddenness, and its impact made her sick with fear. Was that why Mac walked away from his life? Not his brother's death. Not coming to care for this place. None of that seemed enough to make him walk away from everything he'd had in L.A. But what if he had a horrible disease? Some fatal sickness? "Natty, is he okay?"

"No, he's not," the woman murmured, and her expression tightened as she looked at Kate. "He's not okay."

"God, he's dying, isn't he?"

Natty stared at Kate for a long moment, then smiled. "Oh, dear, he probably feels like death warmed over at the moment, but no, he's not dying. Kate, he's hung over."

"Hung over?" He drank too much? Her relief was beyond anything she'd ever experienced. She felt almost giddy with it. "That's it?"

"Right now it is. He never used to drink much, at least not in the past when he was around here. I don't know what he did when he was away. But when he came back this time, he was different, closed off, isolated.'' She shook her head. "I don't know. He's changed.''

"How has he changed?'' Kate asked, seeing an opening to get information, but it wasn't for any story. She simply wanted to understand Mac. On some level she needed to.

Natty reached for a banana from the bowl in the middle of the table and peeled it. She gave half to Tyler and took a bite of the other half herself. Finally she said, ''When he left here, he said he never would come back. Then I got a call one night. He said he was coming home. That was it. He's never told me why.'' She put the banana piece down. "I'm just glad he did.''

"Do you think it's because his brother died?''

"I don't know. Michael died months before Mackenzie came back.''

"Was it because of Tyler?''

"I don't know that, either. He didn't have to come here for the boy. I was here and he knew I wouldn't leave.''

"He could have taken him to L.A., too, couldn't he have?''

Natty frowned. "I guess so, although I don't think a child would have fit in out there.''

So she knew about Mac's life on the West Coast? "Why?''

"He was a sociable person,'' she said. "Single.''

"You mentioned he's a doctor.''

"Oh, yes, he is…or he was. He doesn't practice anymore,'' she said, and Kate could tell that she was editing her words, shutting down. Mac obviously didn't want others to know about his past. "He's ranching now."

"How did he make that transition?"

"I don't know," Natty said. "You're pretty curious, aren't you."

Kate felt heat rise to her face. "I'm nosy, so I tend to ask a lot of questions." She let the toast drop to the plate. "I can be annoying, I know."

Natty smiled. "No, you're not. You're just good at asking questions. Heck, I'd be giving away state secrets to you, if I knew any."

Kate laughed, but her discomfort with deceiving everyone in this house didn't diminish. "I'm not interested in state secrets. I just thought, well, Mac looked so bad this morning, and I thought the worst. I know his brother died, and I put two and two together and got five. I'm sorry."

Natty stood and reached for Tyler to take him out of his chair. She carried him to the sink and started washing his face and hands with a cloth. She spoke with her back to Kate. "It was a car accident. Michael and Janice were on their way back here. They got within ten miles and never made it." She moved back a bit, studied Tyler, then set him down.

"I'm so sorry," Kate said, and meant it.

The instant his feet hit the floor, Tyler was off and running in the direction Mac had gone. "So was I. They were so young and had the little one, too." Natty watched Tyler. "Now he'll never know them."

The boy darted through the door where Mac had

gone, then came back to look up at Natty. "Go Daddy?"

"Not right now, Tyler. Daddy's working." When his bottom lip started to tremble, Natty said quickly, "Why don't you go and get a toy?"

"Missy Boo!" he said, and darted off in the opposite direction, into the hallway, his mind off Mac and onto something else.

"Who?" Kate asked.

"Our cat, Mr. Boo." Natty began taking the dishes to the sink and scraping them into the disposal.

Mr. Boo. "He tangled in your curtains?" She remembered the voice talking about a Mr. Boo. "Tyler chased him? I heard you and Mac talking when I was sick…about your curtains?"

"He ripped them up good." She started water in the sink. "The boy drives him crazy, so he hides a lot, comes out to eat and then hides again, usually in the den. One of Mackenzie's favorite hideouts."

"What does Mac hide from?"

The housekeeper paused in washing the dishes and looked out the window at the snowy day. "My best guess is, he's hiding from life."

Chapter Eight

Kate stared at the older woman. "Why would he want to hide from life?"

Natty started washing the dishes again. "Now that I don't know, dear. I've been trying to figure it out ever since he came back." She rinsed the plate she'd been washing and laid it in the second sink. "I'm pretty good with mysteries, but he's a mystery I can't seem to solve."

If Natty didn't know what was going on with Mac, how would Kate ever figure it out? "Maybe he was just tired of what he was doing."

"Maybe. But how do you stop being a doctor? That's all he ever wanted to be, then suddenly he's not interested."

"Do you think he lost a patient or something?"

Natty actually laughed at that. "No, he didn't. Maybe someone wasn't happy with her new nose, but that's not like a death."

"He was a plastic surgeon?" Kate asked as though she didn't know.

Natty finished the dishes and started draining the sink. "A reconstruction specialist," she murmured.

"So his practice was hardly life and death. I think dealing with Tyler's been more of a challenge to Mackenzie than he's had in years."

"The boy looks like he can be a challenge," she agreed.

Natty dried her hands on the towel that Kate handed her and said, "Actually, there's nothing easy about kids. But they're terrifically rewarding." She folded the towel and set it on the counter. "Speaking of Tyler, do you think you're up to doing me a favor?"

"Anything."

"I need to do a few things, and Tyler needs someone to keep an eye on him. Could you watch him for just a little while?"

"Watch him? I've never baby-sat anyone before."

"Don't worry about it. You don't have to do anything except yell for me if he goes to stick his hand in a light socket or if you think he's going to burn down the house."

"What?" Kate gasped.

"Relax, I'm kidding. You just have to sit with him while he plays, preferably in the living room. He'll watch cartoons or play with his toys."

"Okay, I can try."

She patted Kate's hand. "That's all anyone can ask, isn't it, that you try?"

With that, she took Kate with her to find Tyler. They went through the house, and Kate could see that it was sprawling, with the hallways just beyond her bedroom going out in both directions. Natty led the way through the arched doorway into a huge room that looked as if it spanned the entire front of the house. It was split into two sections—a living area with a massive stone fireplace set between two banks of windows on the side wall and a dining room with dark, antique-looking furniture dominated by a huge breakfront under the front windows.

Tyler sat on the floor in front an overstuffed couch. He was facing the television off to one side of the fireplace, and was surrounded by myriad toys. "He loves building things. He has lots of blocks," Natty said. "I've got beds to change and laundry to do. I can hear you from anywhere in the house, so just yell."

"I sure will," Kate said.

When Natty left, Kate crossed to the little boy. She didn't understand how it had come to this, her being a liar and acting as baby-sitter for a two-year-old. Tyler looked up at her as she reached the sofa, and he held out a plastic airplane to her. She sank beside him on the floor, crossed her legs and took the plane. How hard could this be? Just play with the kid and keep him quiet while Natty worked. "So, it's you and me, kid," she muttered.

Tyler smiled, picked up something else and handed it to her. This time it was a one-legged action figure who looked as if he'd really been through a war. "Thank you," she said.

He picked up more and more, piling cars and plastic people in her lap, then reached for a square wooden block. Before she knew what he was up to, he hurled it at her. She ducked the projectile, but felt it whiz past her cheek. Tyler laughed and she glared at him. "Not nice, not nice at all."

He reached for another block, but she got to it first. She picked it up, grabbed another one and started to stack them in front of him. "They're for building, not for maiming people."

Remarkably, he got the idea. He picked up a block and set it on top of the stack. "That's it, buddy," she said. "Build, don't kill. Blocks are for good things."

"Box," he murmured and reached for another one.

Kate smiled. "You just needed guidance, didn't you."

He looked at her, looked at the stacked blocks, then squealed with glee as he swiped at the blocks. He sent them flying all over, including into Kate. She exhaled and rubbed her arm where one of the blocks hit her. "Do what you want," she muttered.

Two hours later when Natty finally reappeared, Kate was still on the floor with Tyler, partly to keep the kid from climbing up and over the back of the couch, and partly because she was tired and not about to move. "You survived," Natty said as she entered the room and sat on the couch to watch them.

"If you can call it that," Kate said.

"That bad?"

She almost said yes, but didn't. It wasn't *that* bad, not really. Tyler was active and did the most unexpected things, but he was also funny and determined and bright. "No, it wasn't bad."

"I knew you could do it," Natty said.

Kate pushed herself to her feet. "Well, *I* didn't," she murmured, but smiled down at Tyler.

Tyler scrambled to his feet and threw himself at Kate, wrapping his tiny arms around one leg. "Box, box," he said.

She ruffled his hair. "No more blocks, kiddo. Kate's tired." Glancing at Natty, she smiled weakly. "Now I know what Mr. Boo feels like."

"Boo!" Tyler yelled, and took off across the room and out through an archway.

"Don't worry, the last time I saw the cat he was in the kitchen, lying in the side window sleeping, too high for Tyler to reach."

While she'd been playing with Tyler, a part of her had been listening for the back door to open, but it never had. "Has Mac come in yet?"

"Not that I know of," Natty said, and glanced at her watch as she stood. "I don't expect him back for a while. Why don't you go and rest? You've worked hard this morning."

Kate didn't need any coaxing to go lie down. "I think I *will* rest for a bit."

Natty stood. "I'll go and see if I can find Tyler," and she was gone.

Kate went through the arched doorway and heard Natty call out, "No, Tyler, not with the spoon!" She smiled and headed for her room. Before she could reach it, though, she spotted an open door next to hers. She could see shelves filled with books. The den? Mac's sanctuary? She hesitated, then went the door and glanced inside.

The room was smaller than the bedroom. It had

only a single window, a large desk that took up most of the floor space, books and filing cabinets everywhere, and cat hairs clinging to a tweed swivel chair behind the desk. A few days ago she would have not only gone inside, but poked through whatever was lying around to see what she could find. But now she didn't have the heart to do it.

She was tired physically and emotionally. Maybe from being sick, she didn't know. But she had no interest in going through Mac's papers. She left the den, went into her bedroom and closed the door. Maybe she'd feel more like herself later, but right now needed to rest. She climbed onto the bed. She closed her eyes, intending to rest for a bit, then call James again. He'd be dying of curiosity by now.

She fell asleep quickly, and just as quickly, began to dream, weird dreams about Borneo and James and ice and snow. All she knew for sure was that she needed Mac. She had to find him. She looked everywhere, but he was no where to be found. And the cold was there, all around her. She just needed Mac. He could save her. He could stop all of this craziness. All she needed was to take his hand and he could pull her out of this mess. But she couldn't find him. She couldn't even sense him nearby. He was gone. Totally gone.

''Katherine? Katherine?''

Mac. He'd found her. He was there. She opened her eyes and looked up into Mac's face. She scrambled to her knees, reached out to him and wrapped her arms around him. She held on to him tightly. And the fear was gone. The cold was gone. She was okay. She held on for dear life.

"Katherine," Mac said softly, "what's wrong?"

Wrong? Oh, God. It wasn't a dream. She was awake, holding on to Mac. Needing him to hold on to her. If the illusion of a kiss the night before had been crazy, this was insanity. And it wasn't hers to do. It wasn't hers to need him or to hold on to him.

She swallowed hard, then pushed away from him. She made herself look at Mac by the bed and tried to force out words to explain. "I...I was asleep," she said in a low, tight voice as she pressed her hands flat on her thighs. They were shaking and she didn't want Mac to see that.

"A bad dream?" he asked.

She took a ragged breath while her heart hammered against her ribs. "It was a nightmare," she whispered.

"I've had those," he said as he tucked the tips of his fingers in the pockets of his jeans. "Natty used to get me through them when I was kid. You know, the old cinnamon-toast-and-warm-milk routine?"

No, she didn't know. She'd had to get herself through any dreams she'd had as a kid. This was the first time she could remember anyone being there when she awoke in terror. But she lied, just a small lie in the scheme of things. "Sure, of course. Cinnamon toast and warm milk." He didn't include having him hold her. "Why are you here?"

"I came to tell you that lunch is ready, but you were—"

"I'll be there in a minute," she said quickly, not

wanting any descriptions from him about how she'd looked when he found her.

He studied her intently. "Natty told me you pulled kid duty this morning. I couldn't have done it today."

"I survived."

There was the shadow of a smile at his lips. "Yes, you survived the kid. I'm impressed."

She wanted to joke. She wanted to smile back at him, but she couldn't. Not when she was having a hard time forgetting that feeling of being held, the same feeling she'd had when she'd been sick and shaking so hard. "I survived," she said.

"Like I said, I'm impressed. So's Natty." He paused, then unexpectedly reached out and flicked her chin with the tip of his finger. "If you feel okay now, come on out to the kitchen and eat," he said, then headed for the door.

"I'll be right there," she said, but stayed where she was for several minutes trying to stop the shaking that began again as soon as Mac was out of the room.

MAC WASN'T THERE for lunch. He wasn't there for most of the afternoon. She called James, got his machine again, and since Natty and Mac were nowhere around when she left her message, she said, "I'm in his house, and I'm stranded here. I'll call you tomorrow morning and let you know what's happening." She hung up and all thoughts of James were pushed out of her mind when Tyler started to fuss and cry and didn't stop for the better part of the afternoon.

He wanted to be held nonstop, and Natty figured that he was getting some second-year teeth or something. Kate suggested that he possibly had cabin fever. Natty didn't disagree, she just sat down with Tyler on her knee and rubbed something out of a small tube on his gums.

Kate felt useless just watching, and she surprised herself by offering to hold him while Natty took a break. The other woman took her up on it right away. "That's wonderful," she said. "Come sit on the couch and he's all yours."

Kate settled herself on the couch, and fully expected that when Natty gave her the boy, he'd start screaming again. But he didn't. While Natty turned on the television, Tyler snuggled into her. Natty crossed to sit in a chair by the couch and looked at Kate. "Honey, can I ask you something?"

"Sure," Kate said, shifting to get comfortable with the weight of the boy on her arm.

"If you need to talk to someone, you can talk to me."

Kate stared at the woman. "Excuse me?"

Natty leaned toward her, patting her knee. "Mac told me about your dream. That you were pretty upset. Now, if there's something that happened or something you're afraid of, maybe we can help you."

God, no, she didn't want this kindness, this caring. She didn't deserve of it. "I appreciate the offer, but…"

"Are you running away or something? This James

person, is he mean or is he stalking you? Are you in trouble?''

Kate couldn't believe her ears. And she would have laughed it she could have. For the woman was so right. She was in trouble, but it was all her own doing. It came from her lies and being in this house under false pretenses. ''God no. James, he's nice, and I'm not running away. I'm just lost.'' That last word was true. Oddly true. And she'd felt lost for a very long time. But that wasn't what Natty was talking about.

Natty exhaled. ''Okay, if you say so, but I want you to know that I'll listen, no matter what. And Mackenzie can tell you, I can keep a confidence with the best of them.''

''Thank you, that's good to know,'' Kate said.

With that, Natty stood. ''I'll be back.''

After she left the room, the little boy actually went to sleep. Kate shifted again, getting more comfortable, then rested her head on the high cushioned back. She still felt tired, her earlier nap hardly restful. But she wasn't about to go to sleep again, not so soon after those dreams.

She watched television, only half listening to the news. She'd call James tomorrow, but she wasn't sure how much to tell him. Tyler stirred in her arms, sighing softly, and her heart lurched. Things were certainly getting crazy if she was feeling almost maternal with the little boy. Very crazy. Then Natty was back, just as a weatherman was saying, ''And the heavy storms across the Northwestern states are far from over.'' He pointed at a mass of clouds that seemed to be devouring Montana. "Idaho and Montana are looking at more snow and strong winds."

Natty turned off the television, then crossed to Kate and frowned. "So, you've been lying to us from the start."

Kate's guilty conscience kicked in with the speed of light long before she registered that the woman was smiling. Teasing. "How so?" she asked with ridiculously overwhelming relief. She never wanted this woman to know about her lies. She didn't want Mac to know, either. But if she wrote a story, they'd know everything.

She motioned to Tyler. "He's really taken with you. He doesn't let just anyone hold him, let alone get him to sleep, and here you said that you're no good with kids."

As if the boy knew he was being talked about, he stirred again and she thought he'd awake slowly. She was wrong again. He was instantly awake, sitting bolt upright, looking at her, then at Natty. The next thing she knew, he was scrambling off her lap and heading for the arched doorway.

"Talk about waking up perky," she murmured, smiling after him.

"He's a pistol, that's for sure," Natty said. "How do you feel about watching him for just a bit longer?"

Things had gone better than she'd thought they would. No blocks made contact with her head, no catastrophes, and he'd slept like an angel for a while. But looking after him now? He was wound up, refreshed from his sleep and raring to go. "Why?" she asked, not meaning to sound so wary.

"Mac's back out in the barn and someone needs to go out and get him back up here. I was thinking you could watch Tyler and I would go and fetch Mac. I don't think you should be outside, do you?"

Fresh air? Having a few minutes totally alone? That sounded wonderful right then. "How far did he go?"

"Just to the stables, down the back way from the house. Mac cleared it a bit this morning, so it's not hard going. It won't take me ten minutes, tops."

There was a loud squalling sound right then, and before Natty could move, Tyler came running back into the room. He came right over to Kate and stopped in front of her. He held out one little hand, which was closed in a tight fist. Kate grimaced at the gray fur protruding from between his fingers.

"Missy Boo," he said with a smile. "Missy Boo!"

She looked at Natty and spoke quickly. "Just point me in the right direction Mac, and I won't get lost."

"Are you sure?"

Tyler grabbed at Kate's jeans with his free hand, tugging hard enough to make her sway. "Very sure," she said, smiling at the boy, but not about to stay in this house with him and a cat that now must have a huge bald spot. "I need fresh air."

"Okay, there's a jacket of mine in the mudroom you can use. Bundle up good, then follow the cleared path to the first building, the low one. If he's not there, try the barn."

"Cleared path, low building, then barn. Got it," she said, then crouched down in front of the little boy. "Poor kitty," she said. "He's old and slow and you're young and fast. Have pity on the kitty."

He got frowned again, one similar to Mac's, then said quite soberly, "Pity kitty?"

"You got it," she said, and stood. "I'll be right back."

"Take your time." Natty scooped up Tyler. "I'm going to watch my program, the 'most wanted criminals' one."

Kate almost said, "You won't find me there," but settled for, "Interesting."

"You bet. So take your time. You might never have this chance again."

"Excuse me?"

"Unless you get snow like this in California, this might be the only time you get to really enjoy it."

"Oh, yes, sure."

She started back through the kitchen to the mudroom, and heard Natty call out from somewhere behind her. "Try the royal-blue parka and the boots that are on the low shelf."

"Okay," she called, spotting the parka on a hook by the door. She put it on and tugged on the boots. Then she flipped up the hood on the parka and stepped out onto the back stoop. She could see Mac's footprints in the snow, going down some steps and onto a partially cleared driveway. Snow was everywhere else, and the sky was a leaden gray that blocked a lot of the sunlight she'd seen earlier in the day.

A light wind was starting to blow snow back onto the cleared strip. Kate looked up and saw the stables far ahead, and the barn even farther away to the left. Their roofs were heavy with stacked snow, and the trees around them bowed under the weight of the storm's deposits

Kate tucked her chin into the fur-lined collar and started after Mac. She kept her eyes down, watching her footsteps when the going got slippery. The air was so cold it almost burned when she breathed it in, and by the time she got down the winding driveway and neared the stable door, her legs ached and her lungs hurt. Maybe staying with Tyler would have been the better option.

As she stepped under the overhang near the double doors, she found herself smiling. Who would have thought that Katherine Ames, the one with a serious allergy to kids, could have survived this long with a two-year-old in such close proximity? It was a miracle. She chuckled and stamped her feet on the icy tiles to free the snow clinging to her boots and jeans, then reached for the door.

As she touched the strap latch, the door unexpectedly swung out, and in her effort to evade it she was sent backward into a snowdrift. She looked up to find Mac standing over her.

''What are you doing out here?'' he asked as she struggled to sit up.

''What do you think I'm doing? Building a snowman?'' she muttered, twisting to one side to get to her feet.

He reached for her, caught her arm and had her

on her feet in one easy motion. Before she could do more than get her balance, he spun her around and started swiping at her backside. "Then get this straight," he said while she stood absolutely still as she brushed her lower jacket. "You roll snowballs to make a snowman—you don't roll yourself in the snow to make one." With that, he swatted her lightly on her bottom and spun her around. "Got that?"

"Got it," she replied, staring at the man in front of her. He seemed light-years away from the one who'd greeted her in the kitchen this morning or the one who'd held her after the dream. He looked almost easy in his world at that moment. A heck of a lot easier than she felt with him near her.

He pushed his hands into the pockets of his denim jacket, and the Stetson shadowed his eyes a bit as he squinted at her. "Fast learner," he murmured softly.

She looked around, then back at Mac. "What… what have you been doing down here?" she asked.

"Working. I just came to get some fresh air. What are you doing down here? You shouldn't be out in this cold."

"I was looking for you," she said. "Natty wanted you to take a break."

"A break?" he repeated as if it was a crazy notion.

"You know, stop working, rest, relax."

His smile was barely there, but still more than appealing. "I'm familiar with the concept."

"I think Natty wouldn't mind some help with the boy, too. She's watching some television show about criminals."

"Natty and her true-crime shows," he murmured.

"I think she thinks I'm running away or something like that. She wasn't specific, but she let me know that she wouldn't turn me in if I wanted to tell her about it."

"I'll have a talk with Natty." He exhaled. "Right now I've got more work to do. I'll come up later."

She looked around at the ever darkening sky. "What work?"

"Mucking stalls."

"What?"

"Cleaning stalls, then laying fresh hay."

"Oh, of course," she said, and shivered as a cold breeze sprang up to stir the leafless limbs of the trees by the stables. She found it hard to believe that the hands that had made people beautiful could shovel manure. A shiver hit her again, and she felt that weakness in her legs coming back. Mac turned back to his work, apparently expecting her to walk back to the house.

Heading back right then wasn't a good idea. Not until she got some strength in her legs. She'd catch her breath first, then go back. "I've never seen the inside of a stable," she said, and knew how idiotic that sounded. But it was the best she could come up with and not say she was weak and needed his help yet again. She wouldn't do that. "Can I take a peek?"

"Whatever," he murmured, and went on working. She went inside and looked ahead along a central aisle lined about a dozen stalls, each one wood on the lower half and chain-link wire on the top. Only six of them contained horses.

She spotted a gray horse with a white mane closest to the doors, and she remembered an article about Mac that she'd read on the plane. A quote from a girlfriend talking about visiting a ranch in Malibu with Mac. "He's great on a horse," she'd said, then added suggestively, and no doubt with a giggle that the reporter didn't include in the article, "Riding seems like a form of foreplay with Mac."

It had been just another tidbit for the gossip-mongers, she'd thought. But now, in a stable with the man, surrounded by horses and watching him cross to the gray horse to stroke its muzzle, her thoughts were entirely different. Heat flooded through her at the simple action, and she turned from the sight before Mac noticed the change in her expression.

Chapter Nine

"Horses, huh?" Kate heard herself say a bit idiotically.

"Yes, that's what they are, and this is a stable," Mac murmured as he moved down the aisle, glancing in each stall as he went. "And they need fresh hay. I've done some of the stalls. There's just a couple more to do."

She went after him, all the way to the end of the aisle into a large storage space with straw and hay stacked on two walls, sacks of feed on the back wall, along with an array of tools. Mac crossed to the nearest bale of straw, grabbed the bindings and turned, holding it in both hands as he came back toward her. "Since you're here, could you grab a hay fork over there?" he asked as he motioned with his head to the tools.

"Sure, no problem," she said to his back. A hay fork? She went closer to the assortment of tools and found three that looked like forks. Any of them could stab hay, she figured.

"Got that fork?" Mac called.

"Uh…yeah," she said, taking all three of the tools

back with her. She saw Mac moving a huge black horse from a stall on one side to the stall right across from it. He stopped in the middle of the aisle to look at her over the back of the beast. "I just needed the fork," he said.

"Of course," she said, putting the three down by the open door of the stall the horse had just vacated. "I just brought an assortment for you."

Mac put the horse into the other stall, closed the door, then came over to Kate. He reached around her, brushing against her in the process. The not unpleasant smell of hay and horses clung to him. "Didn't know what it was, did you?" he said as he grabbed the closest tool and stood to face her with just inches separating them. He was holding the thing that looked most like a fork. "This is a hay fork."

"Or course, I knew that," she muttered.

"Sure you did," he said, then went into the empty stall. He took off his jacket, hung it on a peg by the door along with his hat, then grabbed the fork and plunged it into the messy straw. He flipped a forkful into a large wheelbarrow in one corner, and when it was full, he turned to Kate. "There's an old saying on a ranch. If you come inside to look, you have to work. You can't just watch someone else work."

"You just made that up, didn't you," she said.

That brought a smile to his face. "Yes, I did, but I didn't think that someone who didn't know what a hay fork was would know that."

"I brought it, didn't I?"

"Sure, along with a pitchfork and an old garden rake."

"I thought you might need the other things."

He gripped the wheelbarrow and started toward the door of the stall. He pushed it to the back of the stables. "If you are going to stay for a bit, open that bale of straw. I need to spread it." He paused and looked back at her. "You can use the pitchfork, the one with sharp tines and the taped handle."

"I knew that, too," she said.

"Of course you did," he said with that smile.

By the time he got back, she had taken off her jacket and managed to get the bail. She was starting to separate the sections of the tightly packed straw. He started to break up the sections, tossing them into the air, watching the pieces settled loosely on the floor of the stall. They worked side by side for a while, spreading the hay, then Mac stood back.

"Done," he said. "Not bad for a city girl."

She looked around. "Not bad for a doctor."

"This isn't brain surgery," he said. "Now move."

"What?"

"I just meant, get out of the stall. I need to put Titan back in here and do the next stall."

She'd thought he was telling her to leave, and she wasn't prepared for how crushed that had made her feel. "Sure, of course that's what you meant," she said, and followed him out of the stall. He led the huge black horse by its leather halter back to his original stall, then shut him inside. He turned to face her. "Thanks for the help."

"It was either this or staying with Tyler for ten minutes." She didn't realize she was going to say that until it came out. Now she tried to backpedal. "I'm sorry. I didn't mean that like it sounded."

He came closer. "Of course you did. Me, too. The kid wears me out. He's so full of energy and curiosity." He smiled a bit at that. "Something you ought to be able to relate to."

His smile was wonderful, especially after the tension from her careless remark about his being a doctor. And with the smile came a scary, unknown feeling she had yet to understand. "I...I'm curious."

"Do you ride?"

"No, but horses fascinate me?"

"Maybe sometime I can teach you to ride."

It was happening, she knew it was happening, but she hadn't had a name for it until right then, when that smile came again. Seduction, that was the word. Just being close, hearing his low voice, that look in his eyes. And he wasn't even trying to seduce her. It was just something her that was being drawn to him even as she tried to fight it. "Me? Ride?"

"Sure, there's nothing like it. Freedom, power. You'd love it."

His idea of foreplay was riding a horse with a woman. God, right then, she felt that mucking out a stall with him could border on foreplay. And she needed to know what was true and what had been her imagination. "I need to ask you something."

That smile teased the corners of his lips. "True to form, aren't you. Questions."

She stared at him and just said it. "Did you kiss me last night?"

He was taken aback, but murmured, "I'm disappointed."

"Why?"

"I always thought if I kissed a woman, she'd at least know she'd been kissed."

She was sure that was true, that is, if the woman was in her right mind and wasn't imagining all sorts of things. "Never mind." She would have left if he hadn't touched her shoulder.

"You're serious, aren't you?" he asked.

She stared at the top button of his shirt. There was no way she could meet his gaze. "Never mind. I...I just need my jacket so I can go back to the house."

He reached over the open top door of the stall and got her jacket off the peg. He held it open for her to put on. With no other option, she slipped her arms into the sleeves. She felt his hands rest on her shoulders for a fleeting moment, then let her go. She turned and almost bumped into him, so close it was almost unbearable for her. "I'll tell Natty you'll be coming up to the house?"

He flicked at a bit of hay that clung to her jacket near her throat, and his fingers brushed her skin. "Sure."

She would have taken a step back and left, but he touched her again, this time with the tips of his fingers on her chin. The soft touch riveted her to the spot. "You don't remember what happened, do you?"

She stared at him. "Did you kiss me?"

"I kissed you," he said, then exhaled, the sound unsteady.

"Oh," she whispered. So it hadn't been a dream, and she didn't know if that was better or worse. She was sane, but he'd kissed her.

"Oh, yes," he said in a low voice, then moved closer, so close she felt his breath on her skin. Then his lips were on hers. She couldn't move. She couldn't think. She just existed for that moment, then the contact was gone. She could see him again, moving back, his eyes searing into hers; then the touch on her skin was gone, and he was farther from her. She fought the urge to touch her lips, either to vanquish the taste of him or capture it. She didn't know which, right then.

"Now you'll remember," he whispered, and even though he wasn't touching her now, it did nothing to lessen his impact on her. "You were leaving? Going to the house? Perhaps you want to call James?"

The mention of James made her stomach clench, and she turned from Mac without a word and headed for the door. She stopped long enough to button her jacket and flip up the hood, then she pulled back the door and left.

Mac watched Katherine go, closing his eyes and flinching when the door slammed shut behind her. Damn it, he was pathetic. Couldn't he be with a beautiful woman without kissing her? The kiss the night before had been one of comfort, of concern. No, that was a lie. He'd thought about kissing her from the first, but that was the best excuse he could come up with. And it was as pathetic as he felt.

After all, Katherine was in a relationship with another man. Mac hardly knew her. But she could tip his carefully reconstructed world out of balance. Now that she'd left, he could inhale again. That was a start. When he saw her later at the house, he'd apologize. Then he'd forget it all when she drove off after Carl got her chains.

At least, that was the plan until he heard the stable door click open. It was Katherine and she stood there with her face flushed and her eyes bright. "I hate snow," she muttered.

He stayed where he was, not trusting himself to move closer to her. "What's wrong now?"

"It's snowing again, I mean, really snowing, like it did before."

He glanced out the high glass-and-wire windows, and it looked dark enough to be night. Snow was falling and he hadn't noticed. "They said it was going to storm again."

"Well, they knew whereof they spoke," she said, not stepping away from the doors. "Now what?"

Titan whinnied shrilly as the wind shook the windows. "Either hike through it or wait. It's your choice."

"Wait?" She sounded as if he'd suggested murder.

"Unless you want to take your chances going back to the house," he said.

She hesitated, and then he heard her sigh. "I guess it's the option thing again, isn't it."

"What?"

"Like the other night. There was one option. Come to the ranch. Now again there's only one option. Stay out here in the stable."

He flinched at the tinge of anger he heard in her voice. "I can get the tractor out and take you up to the house." Then he took back the offer. "No, I can't. It's out of fuel."

"And if I wait and we get snowed in here?"

She had a point. "If we wait and it doesn't let up enough to go up there, I'll hike down to the barn and get some fuel. I'll drive you up. In the meantime, I've got two more stalls to muck out."

She stood very still, then slipped off her jacket. "I'll help." She came toward him, reached for the pitchfork and looked up at him. "Which stall now?"

He motioned to the one next to Titan's. "That one."

Without another word she hung her jacket on a free peg and went into the stall. He watched her for a moment, the memory of the kiss all too fresh in his mind. Along with the movement of her hips, the way her hair swung around her shoulders... His mouth went dry. Damn it, he was like some teenager in the throes of lust. That was it. Lust. And not being with a woman for a very long time. "I'll get the wheelbarrow," he said over his shoulder as he made his escape.

By the time he got back to the stall, Katherine had started stacking the stale hay in the middle of the stall, and he set about putting it in the wheelbarrow. "I called Natty and let her know we were stuck for a while."

She stopped dead and turned to him. "You did what?"

"I called Natty to let her know—"

"You've got a phone down here?"

He couldn't figure out why she was so bothered by a phone call. "In the office."

She blew out a breath. "Then tell me why she let me come down here if she could have just called."

He didn't understand a lot of what Natty did. "I don't know the answer to that."

"Me, neither," she muttered.

"In any case, she said we can have dinner whenever we get back. Meanwhile, she's going to take a nap while Tyler's asleep."

"Sure, he's tired now," she said.

"Natty said you're good with him."

She slanted him a look before getting back to work, tossing the last forkful of hay into the wheelbarrow. "He's got more energy than any ten people I know. I just survived."

Most women would be gushing over the boy. But not Katherine. He got the wheelbarrow out of the stall, tossed in a new bale of hay and broke it open. As they both started spreading the fresh straw, he said, "So, you're not one of those women who can handle ten kids at once and love it?"

"I barely made it through a couple of hours with Tyler," she said without stopping.

He stopped spreading the straw to watch her. "He can be a handful. I told you that."

She glanced at him from under her lashes. "It's more that I'm not very maternal. I guess I take after my mother."

She was a lot of things, and her being maternal or not didn't seem to matter right then. "Your mother?"

"She's not maternal, never was. I suspect she had

a child just for the experience, then found out she didn't like it one bit. But it was too late to take it back." She spread straw as she spoke. "She was stuck with me."

"No brothers or sisters?"

"Good heavens, no. She wasn't about to repeat her mistake."

A mistake? Katherine thought she was a mistake? He'd been angry at James, a total stranger, and now he was angry at a woman who was supposed to be a mother to Katherine. What was happening to him?

"She's a great wife, for what that's worth," she said as she started spreading hay with a vengeance. "And that's not relevant to anything."

"You're going to wear yourself out working like that."

She stopped, breathing hard, then rested the tool against the wall before turning to him. "You're right. I am." She sank onto the fresh hay, crossing her legs and leaning back against the wooden barrier. "And I'm taking a break."

"Me, too," he murmured, and sat down across from her.

Kate closed her eyes for a moment, and her tongue touched her pale lips. The action hit him with the same impact as a blow to the stomach. He could still taste her from the kiss.

"Okay," he said to divert himself. "You're a city girl, an only child from parents who shouldn't have been parents. You're not married, not good in the snow, can't ride horses, can't ski, but you like to watch, you've got a good memory, and you aren't fond of children." He was ticking things off things he knew about her, but inside he was thinking she had the most amazing green eyes and the softest skin and the most wonderful tasting lips.

Her eyes opened and the tension in his middle increased as those green eyes met his. "City college, Cherry Garcia ice cream, Fourth of July," she said, "and type A."

"Excuse me?"

"I went to city college, two years, journalism, no great degree in education. Couldn't afford it and by then my parents were overseas and long gone. My favorite food is ice cream, and when I can afford the best, I splurge on Cherry Garcia. My blood type is A positive. My birthday is on the Fourth of July, but none of the fireworks are for me, and add cream cheese to the list. I hate it. And coffee, which you already know." She stood abruptly. "Now I'm getting back to work."

He hated the talking to stop. No, it was sharing, something he'd never been good at. And it was definitely a first for him since he'd come back. Simple conversation being enjoyable, a give and take. He stood, too. "Okay, back to work," he said, grabbed his pitchfork, lifted a flake of hay and turned to toss it into the corner of the stall. But Katherine stood in its path as the hay flew off the fork right toward her.

It was all over her in the blink of an eye, then she was sputtering, trying to get the hay out of her mouth. She swiped at her face and brushed at the prickly strands that clung to her hair. Mac crossed to her, intent on helping, but when he brushed her shirt, he felt her tense. Then he touched her face, brushing at a strand of hay clinging to a tendril of hair by her ear. Her skin felt soft and silky and warm. The way it had felt when he'd kissed her. And the same need was there, to stroke her skin as he framed her face with both hands.

He caressed her cheeks with his thumbs, and the look in her green eyes echoed the fire he felt in himself. It scared him. He'd always been in control with a woman; even when he kissed Kate, he'd chosen to do so. But now he felt as if he was on some sort of automatic pilot, doing what he wanted, but at the same time knowing he shouldn't. Not when there was a James in the picture, and not when he wasn't fit to ask anything of a woman.

If he was noble, he'd stop it right there. Then she trembled slightly and he knew he wasn't noble at all. "I'm sorry," he whispered, not sure what he was sorry about. He wasn't sorry to be this close, to feel her heat mixing with his, to have her lips so invitingly parted. No he wasn't sorry about any of that.

When her tongue darted out to touch her full bottom lip, he gave up. He didn't allow himself to think about anything except kissing her again and, this time, doing it thoroughly, memorably.

It was a repeat of what Kate had felt an hour ago. Mac touching her, coming closer, that same sense of anticipation until the moment his lips touched hers. When she tasted and felt him, that was where the sameness stopped. This time she didn't stand still, she didn't freeze on the spot. She didn't wonder what was happening, or if she was dreaming again. This time something exploded around her, a need that threatened to consume her, and she moved toward him.

There was no reason, no sanity in the fact that she let him kiss her. Or that she was getting as close to him as she could, or opening her lips in invitation.

There was fire all around, a need that came out of
nowhere, a living thing, and Mac was the only one
who could satisfy that need. His hands were lower
on her, circling her, pressing into the small of her
back, bringing her tightly against his hips. And she
knew that the need was there for him, too.

Somehow her top came loose from her jeans, and
Mac's kisses left her lips, trailing to her throat, to a
sensitive hollow by her ear as his hands spread on
the skin of her back. She trembled, sliding her arms
up to circle his neck, pulling herself higher and closer
to him. Then together they eased back and ended up
in the hay, lying in the sweet freshness. Mac was
over her, twisting to one side, his hands undoing the
buttons on her shirt until her bra was the only thing
between his touch and her naked skin.

She ached for the contact, and when the flimsy
lace was finally pushed aside, she gasped as his hand
found her breast. She heard a soft moaning sound
and realized it was coming from her as pleasure filled
her, rushing into every atom of her being. His lips
followed his hand, tasting her nipple, tugging at it,
and she arched toward him. The sensations overwhelmed her, making her crazy with need, and she
tugged at his shirt, not bothered by a ripping sound,
not as long as she felt his sleek skin under her hands.

Heat and pleasure seemed to be everywhere, kisses
and caresses, his hand slipping into the waistband of
her jeans. The fastener popped, then the denim was
being pushed down. She felt his hand on her stomach, then felt it move lower, lower. Her whole body
tensed with anticipation.

She'd never felt like this before, and the sensation
of neediness almost choked her. She needed this

man. She needed his touch and his heat. She needed him. Everything was shifting, reality being pushed aside by a growing fantasy. It both intrigued her and scared her, but she wasn't going to stop.

Nothing was wrong in this world she was fashioning, nothing, not when Mac stroked her like that, not when she heard his voice, a low rumble, against her heart. In her fantasy, his hand went lower and lower, pushing at her jeans, trying to ease them down and off her hips. And she arched up, trying to help him, trying to be free of her clothes. And she would have been in another heartbeat if a loud ringing sound hadn't echoed through the stables.

The sound cut the fantasy to shreds, and whatever was being built around the two of them in the hay dissolved at an alarming rate. Reality was there. The pleasure was leaving. She heard Mac mutter a jarring profanity about the phone, then he pulled back and looked down at her, coldness starting to invade the space around her.

"Don't move," he breathed as he touched her lips with his forefinger. "Don't. I'll be right back." Then he was up and over her, hurrying out of the stall and toward the phone.

Kate rolled onto her side, embarrassment flooding through her, sickness replacing the pleasure. Struggling to sit up in the hay, she tugged her bra back over her sensitive breasts, then pulled at her shirt to cover herself. No matter how she tried, her fingers wouldn't manipulate the buttons. She got to her feet, pushed the undone shirt into her jeans and redid the fastener.

This was no dream, no hallucination. She'd been ready to do whatever Mac had asked of her. She'd

been ready to act out her own fantasy. She couldn't.
She didn't have right to any of this. She was ready
to get out of there, to grab her jacket and put whatever effort she could summon into getting to the
house in the storm. But she wasn't fast enough. Mac
was back, standing in the doorway of the stall. His
shirt was open, the top fastener on his jeans undone,
and his obvious desire pressed against the rough
denim. He made no effort to hide it. None at all.

He had a cordless phone in his hand and held it
out to her, his expression totally unreadable. "It's
for you."

"Who is it?"

"James. Natty forwarded it down here," he said.

She tried to remain focused as he handed her the
phone.

Reality returned and she remembered who she
was. She worked here for James. She was here for
the story. Not to make love with this man. She had
no right to touch him or kiss him. Her lies could only
go so far. And this was much too far.

Chapter Ten

"This is Kate," she said into the phone.

"Katy, hi," James said. "Was that Parish?"

"Yes." Kate could barely force the words out.

"Hot damn, you did good! I knew you were the right one to put on this. I missed your calls, and I was trying to find the number there. Then Eileen in Research found a connection with the phone company... Anyway, she got it for me."

She closed her eyes tightly and lowered her voice, barely able to endure his excitement. "I'm fine, but it's snowing again, and I...I don't know when I'll be able to leave. The ranch is snowed in completely."

"Hot damn again! You are so good, sweetie. You'll have to tell me later how you did it," he said, and she could almost see him rubbing his hands together greedily. "Is he listening?"

She glanced back at Mac by the door and was jarred by the intensity of his gaze on her. "Mr. Parish brought me the phone."

"I take it he thinks we're together? The woman who answered said something to that effect. 'Oh, you're her boyfriend,' or something."

"Yes, that's the idea."

"Okay, play with that. That should be easy to pull off, since we were together before."

They'd never been "together," not in the way she'd been so close to being together with Mac. "I know. I know."

James was silent for a moment. "Hey, you sound strange."

"What?"

"I told you it was up to you how you handled this. It's your story, your bonus, but is everything okay there?"

"Sure, why not?"

"Tell me."

"No."

"Okay, I get it, he's listening. Say something like, 'I miss you too, honey,' and make sure he hears it."

She looked away from Mac. "No."

"Oh, come on. Play this out. Just say, 'I miss you,' and make him believe it."

"I miss you," she said but the words sounded flat to her.

"Not good, but passable," he said. "Now, for the sixty-four-thousand-dollar question. Did you find out why he did what he did?"

"No," she murmured.

"Okay, you've got time. Call me back as soon as you can talk freely."

"Okay. I'll call tomorrow for sure."

"Call sooner than that."

"I might even be out of here by tomorrow if the storm lets up."

"Damn, I hope not," he said. "You're phenomenal, you know that?"

She felt cheap. "No."

"Believe it," he said, then hung up.

She kept the phone to her ear. "Of course, of course," she murmured. "Me, too," and she hit the off button.

She turned and handed the phone back to Mac, trying not to look at his naked chest or the arrow of dark hair that ran into the waistband of his jeans. "That was James."

"I figured that out when he said his name was James," Mac returned.

She closed her eyes for a moment to center herself, then looked back at Mac. "I'm more sorry than I can say about…about all of this," she said her voice hoarse. "This…this was so wrong and I…I have to go."

He stood very still, the light from the central aisle at his back, shadowing his eyes. "Go where?"

Away from you, she wanted to scream, away from here and away from all of this mess, but instead, she said, "To the house."

"I'll go with you."

She didn't want that, but knew she didn't have a choice. She just wished he'd move away from the door to let her pass. She went toward him, but he stayed put, and she finally said, "Can I get out?"

"You're not a prisoner," he murmured.

"If you say so."

He stared at her, then moved back just enough for her to duck past him. She tried very hard not to touch him, but her elbow hit him in the middle of his bare stomach. "Damn it," she gasped, moving quickly out into the aisle. She grabbed for her jacket, trying to get it on and hoping against hope that Mac wouldn't help her. Thankful that he didn't, she got to the door at the same time she got the jacket on.

Mac was there behind her, his jacket and hat on, and he looked down at her as he pressed one hand to the door. "Storms do strange things to people," he said.

She wished that was what was at fault. "Stupid things," she said, and pushed the door just under his hand.

The door swung open, and she stepped out into the wind and snow. The sky was dark and ominous, the wind made the snow fall almost sideways. Mac raised his voice to be heard. "Follow me. Hold on to the back of my jacket and keep your head down."

She didn't want to touch him, but realized she'd never be able to keep up without holding on to him. She reached for his jacket, caught the hem and held on for dear life as they trudged through the storm. The snow had filled in the cleared swath, and it seemed to take forever for them to get to the house and finally to the stoop.

Mac stopped, turned, grabbed her hand and quite literally pulled her up the buried steps with him. They were at the door, and he pushed it back with his free hand. She all but tumbled into the mudroom and into heat that burned her skin.

"Natty!" he called.

Kate was in the house, safe, and Natty was there,

eyes wide with surprise. Without saying anything, the woman helped Kate out of her snow-damp clothes. Tyler was there, too, running around while Natty took the jacket and helped her pull off the boots. "You poor thing," she finally said as she ushered Kate through the house and into the living room.

There was a huge fire in the hearth, and its heat flooded the room. Natty sat Kate on the couch facing the blaze, then stood over her. "Why did the two of you come in through that?"

Kate looked up at her. "Why did you send me down to get Mac when you could have phoned?"

The woman didn't miss a beat. "Because he wouldn't have come up if I just phoned. It's too easy to hang up and keep working. I thought he'd be more apt to do it for you if you went there because you're the guest."

All he did for her was to make her realize that she was a woman—and a liar. "Well, he's here," she said.

"No, he's not."

Kate twisted to look behind her, but Mac was nowhere in sight. "What the heck?"

"He went back to the stables, something about finishing his work out there, and he never got a meal." Natty looked annoyed. "I swear, he's the most stubborn man."

"Among other things," Kate muttered.

"That boyfriend or yours seems very odd to me," Natty said. "He seemed more interested in where you were, rather than how you were. Is he okay, or is he threatening you in some way?"

Kate shook her head at the absurdity of what the woman was asking her. "Did you see his mug shot on your show today?" she said, trying to lighten the mood.

Natty looked taken aback, then she smiled. "Oh, you're teasing me, aren't you. I know I tend to let my imagination run away with me, but that man, he just didn't seem normal."

Before Kate could try to convince Natty that James was so normal he was boring, Tyler scrambled up onto the couch beside her and tugged on her arm. She looked down at him. "What do you need?"

"Box box." He thrust his hands over his head. "Big box!"

She looked at Natty. "What?"

"He wants to build blocks with you again."

Kate sank back against the soft cushions and moaned, "More building. More destruction."

"That's about it," Natty said. "Why don't I get you something to eat while you help Tyler wreak havoc on his blocks?"

Kate looked at the little boy and found herself smiling. "Okay, blocks it is. You got get the blocks for us."

He didn't need to hear anything else. Before she was done talking, he was off the couch, heading for a big basket on the other side of the fireplace. "I'll call when the food's ready," Natty said, and left.

Kate watched Tyler. The sturdy little boy tugged the basket with all his might and got it to the center of the rug before looking at her with pleading eyes. "Okay, okay, I'll meet you halfway," she said, and slid off the couch onto the floor, then scooted over to where the basket and the little boy were waiting.

Tyler took blocks out of the basket and offered them to her. ''Build,'' he said, and she did as he ordered, stacking one block on top of the other, and trying to forget about the man who'd gone back to the stables.

MAC DIDN'T RETURN to the house until the snow eased up around eight that evening. He stepped through the back door and stopped in his tracks when he heard laughter coming from the front of the house. Tyler. The little boy sounded as if he was having a great time. He took off his outer clothes, hung them up, kicked off his boots, then came into the kitchen. Dinner was still on the stove, a large platter filled with vegetables and roast chicken. No one was in the room. He went through the kitchen, into the hallway and ahead to the living room.

He got to the archway and stopped. Katherine was lying on her back on the area rug in front of the fireplace, and Tyler was sitting on her stomach, clapping and saying, ''Mo, mo!'' Katherine started to bounce him in time with a song she was singing, and Tyler started clapping again and laughing so hard he was almost gasping for air.

Natty came up behind Mac, touched him on the arm and said, ''Tyler's sure crazy about her.''

He never looked away from Katherine, and the anger he felt at James before was replaced by jealousy. She was James's and Mac had no right to mess that up. No right at all. She laughed with Tyler, tickling him, then the two of them rolled onto their sides and she caught sight of Mac in the door. The laughter faltered as she pushed herself up to sit cross-legged, the way she had in the stable. He didn't want to remember that time, so he started talking.

"Sounds as if you're having a good time," he said, crossing past her to the fireplace and, his back to her, holding his hands out to feel the warmth of the flames.

"He's easy to entertain," she said. "Did you get the stalls finished?"

"They're done." He wouldn't tell her how he worked until he felt ready to drop just to keep his mind free of thoughts that were driving him mad. But those thoughts were there now, and he couldn't stop them when he turned and looked at her sitting on the rug. "All done."

"Did your brother work this ranch…before?"

The question startled him. The past had been pushed back and out of the way because of the present. But her words stirred it again. "Yes, he did," he said, and looked over at Tyler, who was scooping blocks into his little wagon. "He loved it."

She appeared to study him from beneath those ridiculously long lashes. "Were you and Michael a lot alike?"

He didn't like these questions and wished he'd stayed at the stables. "No, not at all," he said, sitting down on the raised hearth and leaning forward, resting his elbows on his knees and lacing his fingers together. "Mike was the good one. The one who stayed here and made a life for himself."

Tyler interrupted them, tugging a wagon over to Katherine and demanding her full attention. She helped him build a tower of blocks, watched him knock it over and start all over again. Mac watched the two of them, and something in him started to ache. An ache for what he'd never have. What he didn't deserve and what James would have. A real family. And Katherine. "I hope Tyler grows up to be like Mike." He didn't know where that had come from even as he said the words.

She ruffled the little boy's bright hair. "Natty says he's a real Parish." She looked up at Mac. "So he must be a bit like you. Maybe he'll want to be a doctor, too."

Mac looked down at his hands, not sure what to say, and he was thankful when Natty came back into the room. "Dinner's ready, if you're all hungry."

Mac got up and crossed to Tyler. "Come on, buddy," he said, and lifted him up into his arms. Usually the boy twisted into him, hugging him around the neck, but this time he twisted away from him. He stretched out both arms to Katherine and yelled, "Kay, Kay!" at the top of his lungs.

Kate colored slightly, then reached for him. "Okay, this once I'll carry you, but you've got two legs to walk on." The little boy all but fell into her arms.

Lucky kid, Mac thought, being in Katherine's arms, and followed them into the kitchen. "You carry him like a pro."

"It's the storm, I guess," she said as they crossed

to the table. "It makes you do things you usually wouldn't think you'd do."

He didn't miss the way her voice dropped or the touch of color in her face as she put Tyler in the chair Natty had readied for him. The storm. It all came from the storm. That's what she believed. But he wasn't so sure. He'd never been stormbound with a woman who stirred him in a way he'd thought was gone forever. And he'd never felt less in control with a woman than he did with Katherine. Mac sat down opposite from Katherine who sat by the boy. He could look at her, watch her with Tyler and not be close enough to do anything foolish like touch her. The table was a safety barrier, and he knew how important it was when she looked up from settling Tyler in his chair and met his gaze.

He looked away, taking the food Natty offered and trying to concentrate on the roast-chicken dinner. But nothing changed. Things just got worse. He glanced up at Natty, then Tyler and finally Katherine, all gathered at the big table, the two women talking, the child mashing his roasted potatoes with his fist, and it struck him that they almost looked like a family. That stopped him dead. No, they weren't a family. They were his brother's child, a housekeeper and a stranger.

He concentrated on eating until he felt Katherine's eyes on him. He met her gaze and she looked away quickly. Color touched her cheeks again, and he knew that she hadn't forgotten what had almost happened in the stables. He wished he could forget.

"What...what's the latest on the weather?" she asked Natty.

"Still coming down," Natty said, "but it's expected to stop pretty soon. Then it's clear sailing when the plows get done."

"How soon will the plows get the roads cleared?"

Natty looked at Mac. "Tomorrow morning?"

"Probably." He looked right at her and said something that he was sure would keep things in perspective. "James will be glad to get you back, won't he?"

The color came again. Damn it, how long had it been since he'd seen a woman blush? "Yes, I guess he will," she said.

And she'd leave. That only showed him how empty his life could be. "I've got work to do."

"Not in the stable at this time of night, surely," Natty said.

"No, paperwork." He headed to the den, went inside and closed the door. There was no work, but there was a bottle of whiskey. He crossed to the desk, sat in the swivel chair and opened the bottom drawer.

The bottle was there, half-full, with a glass by it. He looked at, started to reach for it, then drew back and slid the drawer shut. Getting drunk wouldn't solve a thing.

KATE TOOK THE FIRST easy breath she could manage since looking up and seeing Mac watching her playing with Tyler.

"Are you okay?" Natty asked.

"Fine." A perfect lie to follow her making a perfect fool of herself with Mac. She cringed at the willingness she'd displayed when he touched her. Pushing back her plate, she said, "This was delicious, but I'm stuffed."

"Beats me how you keep any meat on your bones with as little as you eat." Natty stood, taking the plates to the sink and talking over her shoulder. "Men used to like fuller women." She came back to the table. "My Norman, God rest his soul, liked meat on the bones, and I was happy to oblige."

Kate smiled. "Norman was a lucky man. You're a wonderful cook and do such a great job around here."

She shrugged. "It's as natural to me as breathing, being here with Mackenzie and the boy." She started clearing the mess Tyler had made, handing him half a roll to keep him busy while she worked. "They're like my family."

"What about Tyler's grandparents?"

"Gone. I don't know what happened to Janice's parents. But she was pretty much alone when she met Mike. She came to Bliss to paint, met Michael and that was that. She never left."

"Love at first sight?"

"Absolutely." Natty looked at her. "Do you believe in love at first sight?"

Kate shrugged. "I'm not sure I believe in love, let alone love at first sight."

Natty looked shocked. "What about James? I thought you said…? No, I assumed that you two were serious."

Kate felt cornered by her own lies, and she tried

to think back to when she and James dated. "I liked...I like him. He's really great. Nice. Ambitious." She tried to joke her way out of it. "And he's got great dimples."

Natty didn't laugh. "You don't love him, though, do you."

Why was she talking about love with this woman? "I told you, he's great," she said, and hoped that would end it.

"Hmm," Natty said, wiping Tyler's hands. "I see."

"You see what?"

"Honey," she said, lifting the boy from his chair and setting him down on the floor to run loose, "you'd know it if you were in love, trust me. You wouldn't be able to think about anyone else. You wouldn't want to be with anyone else." She smiled slightly. "And something most people won't tell you, being in love is the most uncomfortable condition in this life. You're on edge, nervous, you feel crazy, off balance, but you don't want it to end."

"That sounds like a *condition,* not love," Kate said.

Natty started across the room, following the boy, who'd ducked out into the hall. "I guess it is," she said, pausing by the door. "But when it happened to me and Norman, I just didn't care," she said with a grin, then went after Tyler.

Nervous? Edgy? Crazy? Off balance? That certainly described the way she felt around Mac. No, that was crazy. That was all wrong. That wasn't right at all. It couldn't be. She stood quickly, leaving the empty kitchen and heading for her room.

Once inside, she closed the door, then leaned weakly back against it. "No, no, no," she muttered to herself. That wasn't even remotely possible. The doctor playboy and the liar journalist? That wasn't going to happen. "Not in this lifetime," she muttered to the room.

MAC SAT IN THE DEN behind the huge old desk his father had once used. The desk Mike had used. Now he was using it. The snow beat on the window over the desk, and the wind shook the panes. He slowly swiveled in the chair, not bothering with any lights other than the goosenecked desk lamp.

He caught a flash of movement out of the corner of his eye and barely had time to brace himself before Mr. Boo jumped at him. The big gray ball of fur made a perfect landing in Mac's lap, then looked up with inscrutable amber eyes. "I could use a warning sometimes," Mac complained as he stroked the cat's head.

A banging on the door startled him and the cat. Both froze for a second, then both heard Tyler yelling, "Boo!"

The cat darted a look at Mac as if to say, "Protect me."

"Don't worry, the door will hold against him." Right then the banging stopped and Mac heard Natty saying something to the boy, then the sound of footsteps moving away from the door. Mac exhaled, and Mr. Boo curled up in his lap. Just when peace

seemed within reach, Mac heard a door close, probably Katherine's bedroom door, then a soft bumping
sound. Whatever peace he'd hoped for in here was
gone completely when images of Katherine refused
to go away. "Damn it," he muttered, and the cat
scrambled off his lap and jumped onto a file cabinet
on the far wall.

Mac opened the desk drawer, took out the half-
full bottle of whiskey, picked up the glass, then
kicked the drawer shut with his foot. He poured some
of the amber liquid into the glass, then leaned back
in the chair and took a sip. The alcohol burned a path
down his throat before the heat settled in his middle.
He stared out the window at the snowy night.

When he'd come back last year, it had been storming, but then it had been rain, sleeting, driving hard
across the land. A perfect backdrop to his misery.
Now the snow and cold seemed fitting. He looked at
the clock. It wasn't even nine yet. The evening
loomed ahead of him. He took another sip and settled
low in the chair.

Chapter Eleven

Mac looked up at the sound of a soft knock on the door. Natty slipped into the room, without Tyler. "What's going on?" Mac asked.

"Tyler's down, hopefully for the night, and I'm going to watch television. Do you need anything?" She glanced at the drink in his hand. "Coffee?"

"I'm fine," he said. "What about her?"

"Her?"

"Katherine. What's she doing?"

"She's in her room. I was going to ask her to watch TV with me. Why don't you join us?"

"I've got paperwork."

"So I can see," she said. "Don't drown yourself in it."

"Natty, don't you start."

"I was here before you left, and I was here when you came back. All I can say is, before you left, you never would have drunk yourself into a stupor."

"I don't drink myself into stupors."

"You were hung over yesterday morning."

"I was tired. I don't sleep well and—"

"Never mind. You do what you have to do."

He sat back and ran his free hand over his face. "That's what I'm trying to do."

She crossed the room and crouched down by him, her hands resting on the arm of the chair. "Mackenzie, you're doing a good job for us, but what about yourself? You don't sleep well. You hardly ever smile. I think seeing you smile with Kate is the first time that's happened in—" she shrugged "—a very long time."

God, he didn't need this now. "Don't."

"What? Say that a pretty woman could make you happy?"

"Don't think that what Mike had is what I want or need."

"Wasn't there anyone you met in California you thought about settling down with?"

"No." And that was true. He'd never found anyone that he wanted to stay around for longer than a few dates. "No one."

"That's too bad."

"Just let it be," he said, fingering his glass.

"Okay," she said, and stood. "Kate will be gone tomorrow probably."

"We weren't talking about Katherine, were we?"

"No, of course not. Besides, she's got a boyfriend."

"Exactly."

"So that's settled," she said, patted him on the shoulder, then turned and left.

Mac gripped the glass in his hand tightly. If he'd stayed here and never left, what would he be now? What would he be thinking and feeling and doing?

Who would he be doing it with? He shook his head.
He hadn't stayed. He'd left for medical school and
never looked back. Fifteen years in all before he'd
come back to stay. Fifteen years that just seemed like
a blur now. Ending with that moment when he knew
he had to come back here. He thought he'd known
who he was, then he'd lost it all. He drank the last
of the whiskey, but didn't refill the glass. Maybe
there wasn't anyone to find.

KATE DIDN'T COME OUT of the bedroom for an hour,
and by the time she did, Mac was nowhere in sight,
and Natty was in the living room watching television.
The older woman patted the sofa by her and smiled.
"Sit and look at this."

Kate crossed and sat by the woman on the sofa,
curled her legs under her and looked at the television.
The picture of a surly man with tattoos all over his
neck and even on his face, filled the screen. A mug
shot from some police department. The voice was
talking about a three-state manhunt and a reward.

"There aren't any weather report on?" Kate
asked.

"I'll look in a minute. First I want to see the update on this guy." When a voiceover said, "Update.
After a tip from a viewer, Billy John Sowers was
found trying to leave the country at the Mexican border and is now in custody awaiting arraignment."

"That's great," Natty said, then sat back and lifted
the remote. "Justice is served and someone got a
huge reward." She pressed a button, and the weather

channel came on. "Oh, my," Natty breathed. "Look at that storm front."

Kate watched the weatherman motion to gray clouds that were hovering over most of the Northwestern states. "Scattered storms on the Oregon/ Washington coast, heading inland to join the storms already pounding Utah and Montana," he said. "It will be moving through quickly, so the holiday should see sun by the afternoon. Travel isn't good, but the turkey should be."

Kate stared at the screen as a huge cartoon turkey overlapped the map above the words, "Happy Thanksgiving."

"Thanksgiving?" she asked.

"Tomorrow," Natty said.

"Oh," she said, sinking back in the couch. "I forgot."

"You're far too young to be having a 'senior moment' about something like Thanksgiving," Natty said on a chuckle.

"We didn't do much for holidays when I was a kid, and I still don't," Kate said as she looked at the older woman.

"Well, I've always made a fool of myself for any and all holidays." Natty frowned slightly. "Although Mackenzie sort of put a damper on last Christmas, just getting home and trying to adjust."

That was an opening and Kate took it. "He came back here just to look after Tyler?"

"You sound as if that's crazy."

"Oh, I didn't mean that, but why didn't he just provide for him? You know, pay for whatever he needed and check on him now and then? You're here, or he could have hired someone.'' She herself had had untold numbers of baby-sitters and nannies when she was growing up. ''He would have been well cared for.''

Natty frowned at her. ''That's warehousing a child. And Mackenzie, despite everything, knew that Tyler needed family. I suspect that Mackenzie needed that family, too.''

''He gave up everything he had out in California to come back here to the ranch just for Tyler?''

Natty's frown deepened. ''What do you think he gave up?''

She'd spoken without thinking. But she just wanted to understand Mac. ''He was a doctor and doctors tend to have quite a life. And he's not a doctor here.'' She shrugged. ''I just assumed…''

Natty frowned. ''That he gave up a lot. I assume he did, too. But I told you I believe in fate. This world isn't all random acts. At least I don't think so.'' She touched Kate's hand, a warm contact. ''Just look at you. You getting lost, and Mackenzie happening to find you, and you having to stay here for a few days—that isn't all just some quirk. It's all for a reason. Maybe it's to give you time to breathe a bit, or to look at what you've got, or to maybe reevaluate your life.''

That hit a nerve, a very raw nerve in Kate at that moment. Reevaluating her life? There was a lot to at least re-think. Being away from the world she was submerged in, day in, and day out, was making her think, but mostly about the lies. They didn't sit well with her at all. Even justifying them as a means to an end, didn't work for her at that moment. She wasn't sure what they were going to cost everyone in the end. She looked at Natty. "You think so?"

Natty nodded. "Yes, I do. And as I said before, if you want to talk about anything, I'll listen. And it won't go any farther. That's a promise."

Right then Kate had the craziest notion just to tell Natty everything, get it all out in the open. If anyone knew how to make this right, it was this woman beside her on the couch. If anyone knew how to stop the craziness that was threatening to suffocate her, Natty would. All Kate had to do was tell her the truth. That was all.

"Do you want to tell me something about yourself or about your life?" the woman asked.

The urge was so strong to be honest that it all but choked Kate. The words were there, so close to being said, but they were stopped.

"What about your life?" he asked as he appeared at the side of the sofa.

Kate looked over at him, and as she met those narrowed hazel eyes, she knew that under different circumstances, at any other time, she wouldn't lie to him. That wouldn't be an option. But as he'd said before, there were no options. And telling Natty anything wasn't an option. The craziness faded even more. Sanity took its place and the world steadied for her. She clasped her hands in her lap and looked down at them. " My life? At the moment, it's all about being stuck here," she said. "And now I found out tomorrow is Thanksgiving."

Mac moved to the overstuffed chair angled near the fireplace and sat down. "Thanksgiving?" He looked at Natty. "Are you sure?"

"Boy, between the two of you, the holidays are in serious jeopardy," the housekeeper said. "Yes, I'm sure tomorrow is Thanksgiving."

He sank back in the chair with a rough sigh and rested his hands on the soft fabric of the arms. "I guess we can't change that," he murmured, and glanced at Kate with hooded eyes. "That's why you were going to Shadow Ridge—for the holiday?"

The lies went on. She nodded. "The holiday."

"That you managed to totally forget?" Natty asked.

She glanced at the older woman. "I'm afraid so."

"You really don't celebrate the holidays, do you."

"No, I don't," she said, and kept her gaze from swinging to Mac. Just his sitting there was making her uneasy, bringing back what had almost happened earlier in the stable.

"What about Christmas?" Natty asked.

Kate shrugged. "No." Work, not their daughter, had always been the center of her parents' life. The old loneliness was there, and it wasn't welcome. She didn't belong in this room any more than she belonged anywhere. She stood. "I'm tired. I think I'll go to bed." The madness that had taken over when she'd almost told Natty everything was shifting into something that was leaving a bitter taste on her tongue. "Maybe tomorrow the roads will get cleared."

"Don't count on it," Mac said, and she had to look at him.

"It stopped snowing. Why wouldn't they be?"

"Sorry, but it's the holiday. They won't do much except possibly clear the main street in town and eat turkey."

If her presence here had just been about a story, she'd be rejoicing about the extra time. Now her time here was just being prolonged until she could get back to Los Angeles and tell James that the only story was about a lonely man and little boy without his parents. Hardly earth-shattering news.

"Good night," she murmured, and headed toward her bedroom. She should call James, but she couldn't make herself get out the cell phone and try to put in the call. Tomorrow she'd try, she decided, then changed into the nightgown and got into bed.

SOMETHING STARTLED KATE out of a dreamless sleep. She awoke to a room with moonlight filtering in through the frosty windows. The storm was over. Maybe that was what woke her. The total silence. Whatever it was, she couldn't go back to sleep. She got out of bed and headed to the kitchen to get a drink, but stopped at the kitchen door.

The only light in the room came from above the sink, but she didn't have any trouble making out Mac by the back door, hunkered down, picking up something that was scattered on the floor. "What in hell are you doing up?" he asked without looking at her.

His tone was abrupt and laced with annoyance.

''What in hell are *you* doing up?'' she countered, staying in the doorway.

He stood and that was when she saw he had a book in his hands, and he was pushing some paper into it. ''Taking care of things.''

She glanced at the clock. ''At three in the morning?''

''Whatever.''

She had no idea where the crackling hostility came from. ''Now that's an unresponsive response.''

''Whatever,'' he muttered again.

One look at Mac and she realized a truth. Instead of digging for the story, if there was a story, she'd been pulling back for quite a while. As if she didn't want to know the truth. And that made no sense whatsoever. Mac moved, crossing to the table, and she watched him. The dim light did little to alleviate the dark shadows under his eyes or show what sort of book he had in his hands. ''I came to get a drink,'' she finally said as he tossed the book onto the table.

''Don't let me stop you,'' he murmured as he opened the book again, and started sorting through whatever he'd dropped on the floor.

She crossed to the sink, found a glass and got some water, then turned and saw Mac standing by the table. She started to leave, but as she neared the table, she could see that Mac was stacking snapshots. She stopped by him. ''Pictures?''

He didn't respond, but pushed his hand into his pocket, then turned to give her something. It was her canister of pepper spray. The metal was still warm. ''Where did you find this?'' she asked.

"By the truck," he said, then crossed the room to the cupboards by the sink.

She stared at the shiny cylinder in her hand. "Thanks."

She heard the sound of glass clinking on glass, then looked up as Mac came back toward the table. She was certain he'd go right past her and out of the room, but he didn't. He dropped down in a chair and set his glass on top of the photo album.

"Do you need more light to look at that?" she asked, motioning to the book.

"I'm not going to look at it." He took a drink of the amber liquid in his glass. "They're just pictures. My parents were obsessive about taking pictures."

"You're lucky," she said. "You can see the past right in front of you, instead of depending on your memory. All I have are school pictures. I'd love to have a book full of memories, something to remind me of what happened years ago." She took a sip of her water, then put the glass down. "You're lucky," she repeated.

"Sure," he muttered. "I'm lucky."

She'd said the wrong thing, but she didn't know why. "Well, you are." She motioned to the book. "You've got memories, good memories. I'd give anything to have that." Until she said those words, she didn't realize how true they were, how painfully true. She would have given anything to have family who really cared and a book full of memories of good times.

Without looking away from her, he picked up his glass, then pushed the book closer to her, almost sending it off the side of the table. "If you want them, they're yours." With that, he stood and would have left if she hadn't gone after him and said, "What are you doing?"

He stopped at the door, then looked back at her, his eyes shuttered. "I told you, you can have them. I don't want them."

She picked up the book and went closer to him, holding it out to him. "They're yours."

She saw him take a rough breath, the action making his shoulders shudder. "I don't want them."

"What are you talking about?"

"You and your damn questions," he whispered hoarsely, ignoring the book.

"Mac, I just want…" She didn't know what she wanted, except to stop the pain she saw in his eyes. "Why did you ever come back here?"

Without warning he reached out and touched her cheek with the tips of his fingers. Cold fingers. Unsteady fingers. "Don't go down that road. Just say good-night, Katherine, and go to bed."

She should have. She would have. But she couldn't. She didn't move. "And what about you?"

He drew back from her. "I'll survive."

She'd been alone for what seemed most of her life, but the man in front of her was beyond that. He wasn't just alone. He was cut off and isolated in a way she couldn't begin to understand. "If you want to talk—"

He cut her off. "Oh, God, no, don't do that."

"I'm just trying to—"

"Get answers?"

She wanted desperately to understand what was going on with him. And right then, it had nothing to do with a story. "I guess so," she admitted, her voice barely a whisper.

"Why, so you can give me sympathy? Tell me how sorry you are?"

"No, so I can understand."

"Good luck. If you understand, that'll make a grand total of one." He turned from her and walked away, heading down the hallway.

She just stood there. She didn't have any idea what had just happened or why. But she felt drained. She was still holding the book, with its brown plastic cover that simply said, "Photos."

She hesitated, then went back to the table and opened the album. In the low light she saw pictures of people she felt she knew, though she'd never met them. Mac's mother, a small woman with a smile that was reminiscent of his. His father, a man who looked a lot like him, or maybe what he'd look like in the years to come. And Mike. A young boy with a grin, a mop of thick hair and standing by his older brother.

She looked down at Mac, maybe ten years old, in a cowboy outfit that matched his brother's. A huge Christmas tree behind him. His hands on his brother's shoulders. Memories. Wonderful glimpses of what had been. Her eyes stung with unshed tears. A family. Mac had had it all. Then he'd left, gone off, leaving it all behind. Now he was back, the three people gone, the smile gone, and in its place, bitterness and pain.

Maybe it was the loss. Maybe that was what it did to people. She didn't know. It hit her that she wasn't close enough to anyone to feel that sort of pain and grief. She swiped at her eyes, then picked up the book and held it to her. She didn't know which was worse, having something and losing it, or never having it at all.

Kate headed back down the hallway with the book but went right past her bedroom. She went toward the den and saw a light on under the closed door. The weight of the book in her arms kept her from going away and leaving him alone. He needed the book. It was his. Not hers.

She rapped softly on the door. There was no response, so she knocked again. Finally she heard a scuffing sound, then footsteps and the door opened. Mac stood in front of her, his shirt gone, and the jeans his only clothes. She had to force herself not to remember the feeling of his chest under her hands, and not remember him touching her.

She held out the book to him. "This is yours."

He stared at it as if it were a poisonous snake, but when she continued to hold it out, he finally took it. He dropped it on a shelf by the door, then turned to at her. "Anything else?"

Words came, words she'd never said to anyone, but this man had the ability to make her think and feel things she'd never thought or felt before. "I've never had a real family. I've got a mother and father, such as they are, but no brothers or sisters, not even aunts and uncles or any baby-sitter who gave a damn about me. My parents didn't take enough photos to bother putting in an album.

"They didn't try to make a home. We lived in furnished apartments. Easier to leave, which they did. They left all the time. If someone told me to go home, I wouldn't even know where to go. It's not Borneo, and it's not even Los Angeles. You've got this place. You've got Tyler and you've got Natty. You've got a real home."

As she spoke, her words stunned her, yet the truth in them was strong. She looked at Mac, at the man she'd come here to find, the man who'd found her. The man who was making her see how little she had in her life. "You don't know how lucky you are, despite everything," she whispered. "You're here and you hate it. You've got everything." She swallowed hard and her eyes were starting to sting with unshed tears. She hated tears and fought them. "Why are you even here?"

He'd stood there motionless while she spilled everything out, and when she took a shaky breath, he grabbed her arm and pulled her into the den. She had no idea what was happening until he let her go, closed the door and turned to her, still keeping his grip on the doorknob. "Okay, okay, that's enough," he said, looking angry now. "Stop it."

She glared back at him. "What? You're mad that you have to be here, that you have that little boy who adores you? That you have a housekeeper who's more of a mother to you than I ever had? That I'm…" She stopped on a gulp. No, she wasn't going to finish that. There was no way she'd say that she knew she was going beyond mere concern with him, way beyond. ''Quite a burden, huh?''

His eyes narrowed as he moved closer and grasped her by the upper arms, his hold hovering just this side of pain. ''Burden? You don't know what you're talking about. But I'll tell you, and I'm only going to say this once. Then I won't ever say it again.'' He let her go just as abruptly as he'd grasped her. ''Then you'll leave me the hell alone about it,'' he ground out.

She stayed right where she was, fighting the urge to rub her arms.

He took a ragged breath, then uttered in a low, rough voice, ''I'm here because I'm responsible for Michael's death.''

His words hung between them, and in some weird way Kate was waiting for the punch line, the joke in it all, no matter how macabre it was. But it never came. He was serious, painfully so. He was handing her an unbelievable story, the one she'd came to find, and all she wanted to do was make him take back the words. ''No, that's not true,'' she breathed.

He brushed past her to go farther into the room. ''Now get out,'' he said.

She turned as he dropped down in the swivel chair at the desk, then reached for a liquor bottle and a glass that sat on top of a clutter of papers. He had them both in his hand, then put them down with a thud. ''Damn it,'' he said and sank into the chair with a shuddering sigh.

''It can't be true.''

He jerked, as if startled that she was still there, but

he didn't turn to look at her. He sat forward, put his elbows on the desk and buried his face in his hands. "I might be a rotten bastard, but I'm not a liar." His muffled voice made the skin rise on her arms, his words hitting close to home.

She stayed where she was, not daring to go closer, when all she wanted to do was grab him and shake him. "No, no. Natty said it was an accident, that they had an accident, and she never mentioned anything about you having anything to do with it. Nothing."

"She doesn't know."

"You *are* drunk, aren't you?"

He laughed, a humorless sound that made her feel even worse. "No, I'm not drunk. Being drunk doesn't help, anyway. It's never changed the facts."

She didn't know what to do. Let it stop right there or finish this. If he kept talking, James would be thrilled. What a story—Mac responsible for his brother's death, and in guilt and remorse, had walked away from the golden life. The doctor had killed his brother. She'd be able to write her own ticket after this. But no excitement materialized. No thrill at her brilliance getting him to talk. Her heart lurched at the way his shoulders hung forward.

"My God, Mac, you can't mean—"

His hands hit the desk. "Stop!"

If she'd seen pain in him before, it looked ready to consume him now. This was destroying him, and a story would finish the job. Right then, she knew what she'd do. Nothing. She wouldn't. She couldn't. It was simple. There was no way she could do anything to hurt this man, or Natty, or the boy. And anything she wrote, no matter how sympathetic or nonjudgmental, would hurt everyone.

She'd come for a story. She'd found it. Natty had talked about reevaluating her life. She'd just decided to reach past that and go against everything she'd ever held to. She was going to walk away from the story of a lifetime.

Chapter Twelve

Kate had been about to leave the room. She didn't want to hear anything more, but Mac began talking again and she was compelled to stay. It was as if something was crumbling in him, and the words were there, void of any emotion, but powerful in their content. "Mike came to save me and he died because of it." Mac didn't move as he spoke, just stared straight out the window into darkness. "There I was, his big brother, the golden boy of my social circle, a real go-getter with my practice that catered to the rich and famous. There were a lot of perks in that life, parties, being a celebrity of sorts, fringe benefits that I never thought about turning down. Lots of fun. Lots of parties. No limits.

"And I never thought about this place Mike was holding together, keeping going. I was well past that. I'd left this all behind and gone on to what I thought was the perfect life, until I'd gone too far in just about everything."

She inched forward silently until she was by his side, able to see his profile, and only realized then that his eyes were closed. He was watching his own memories in his mind. Painful memories.

"Mac, you don't have to do this," she whispered when he took a ragged breath.

He went on as if she hadn't spoken. "Mike and Janice came to L.A., left Tyler with Natty. Mike was worried about me and wanted to bring me home. He said that I'd lost myself somewhere, and this person I'd become wasn't his brother. I resented and hated every word he said. I was successful, doing better than any Parish ever had, and it had nothing to do with sweat and manure. A real success story. But he didn't buy that.

"He'd heard things, and he was scared for me. Hell, I wasn't scared." He exhaled and Kate saw his hands curl into fists. "I didn't have the good sense to be worried about what I was doing. He tried to coax me into coming back here, to take some time off, to take a hard look at my so-called life. To re-evaluate that life."

"He cared about you," she said softly.

His knuckles were white now. "I know. I know." He opened his eyes. "But I was so damned self-involved that I couldn't see that. We got into a fight to end all fights. I told him to get the hell out of my life, that I didn't need a brother like him. That as far as I was concerned, I didn't have a brother." He shook his head as if he could ward off the pain and memories. "Then he was dead."

"It was an accident," she said.

"Yes, technically. I fought with him, threw him out, and the only reason he was even on that road that night was because he knew that Mackenzie Parish was lost and he couldn't get him back.'' He scrubbed a hand over his face. ''It took me three months to figure out that Mike had been closer to the truth than I'd been for years. Mackenzie Parish was lost. I came back to try and find him, and somewhere along the way, I made a promise to do what I could to make up for what had happened…especially to Tyler.'' He exhaled. ''I'm here, doing penance, trying to make up for the unforgivable.''

She had her story. Simple and horribly painful. ''I'm sorry,'' she murmured, because she couldn't think of anything else to say.

''Aren't we all?''

He stood, and she touched his arm, as if she could help him hold it together with that simple gesture. She knew he was in real danger of falling apart after exposing all his guilt and his grief. She was in danger of falling apart herself.

As he looked down at her hand on his arm and she was prepared for him to move away from her. Instead, he pulled her toward him and simply held her. She closed her eyes tightly and listened to his heart beat against her cheek. In that moment one thing was painfully clear. If she let herself, she could love this man with a fierceness that caught her breath in her chest.

It was no longer just a possibility; it was verging on a fact. She couldn't stop it from snowballing with each beat of his heart. It took on a life of its own and brought an ache to her soul, both for Mac and what he was enduring, and for what she knew could never be. He took a ragged breath, and things escalated.

She was falling in love with him. It was simple. It was clear in her mind and heart. Love at first sight? Maybe Natty was right. It was crazy and painful and nerve-racking and scary.

And she wanted nothing more than to take away his pain. ''Mike loved you,'' she whispered. ''The accident wasn't anyone's fault.'' His arms tightened around her, and there was a shuddering release of breath. ''You have to forgive yourself, Mac, and let go of the guilt.'' She knew all about guilt.

His chin rested on her head, and when he spoke, his voice was a low rumble. ''What do you know about guilt?''

''More then you think.''

He held her back, his hands on her shoulders. ''About all you're guilty of is being a good listener, getting me to say things I haven't said out loud to anyone until now. And for being...'' His eyes roamed her face. ''For being beautiful in that horrible nightgown.'' His smile was unsteady and gone before it had barely begun. ''Beautiful,'' he whispered, and leaned toward her.

When the kiss came, it was unlike any other kiss she'd ever shared in her life. The connection was there, and an all-encompassing sense of completeness. He was there. She was there. They were holding each other, and in that moment, it was enough to just connect, to hold to each other and be there for another person. All the isolation she'd felt was gone for that instant. All that sense of being alone in the world. Gone.

And she knew what it meant to love another human being. She knew what it meant to touch another soul. To feel what that soul felt, to want to heal all the hurts and take away all the pain. He moved back, but she stayed very still, almost unable to take in what had happened. What was happening. She loved him. But she would never tell him. It was that simple.

His hands lifted to frame her face and she saw the brightness in his eyes. The way he had to swallow hard to be able to speak again. "Thank you," he said, the words coming out in a tight whisper. "Thank you."

Her world was upside down. Everything had shifted, and what she'd been before that moment was gone. She had to tell him the truth. "Mac, I..." was all she could manage around the tightness in her throat.

He glanced at her lips, then met her gaze again. "Tomorrow," he said, and kissed her quickly, fiercely, before he let her go. "Tomorrow," he murmured again. "I need to think, to sort through this."

Truth be told, she did, too. She had to figure out how to say what she had to say, and she had to figure out what to do if the truth destroyed what she'd just discovered. "Yes, okay, tomorrow," she whispered, then turned.

She got as far as the door before Mac spoke her name. "Katherine?"

She stopped, but didn't look back. "Yes?"

''Picking you up in the storm is one of the smartest things I've ever done,'' he said.

She nodded, words not there for her now. She went out, closing the door quietly behind her, and stood in the hallway for a long moment. This was love? This disorientation? This confusion? This ache? The joy of finding it and the fear of what it could do to her and the fear of it being gone before she could even touch it? She hugged herself and walked quickly back to her room.

She got into bed, turned out the light and made a promise to herself. No matter what happened, no matter how things went from now on, there were no more lies. She'd talk to Mac tomorrow, lay everything out, explain it to him, do everything she could to make him understand where the old Kate had been coming from. Mac would know who Katherine Ames really was, and what happened after that was up to him.

MAC HADN'T SLEPT all night, but not for the usual reasons. This time it hadn't been Mike who filled his thoughts, but Katherine. What happened with her. What he'd done, telling her everything, waiting for her to recoil in horror, then finding only understanding and caring. It had stunned him and given him a hope that he could live with what he was, with who he was. That it was possible to live again.

Katherine. He'd wanted so badly to hold her and feel anchored again. What she'd given him last night had been precious. Her being there. Her understanding. Letting him hold her. Letting him feel grounded.

Even if she was with James, she'd begun a healing in his soul. He wanted to talk to her, to see her and touch her, but he didn't know what he'd say now. He didn't know what she was offering him. Not with James in the picture. That was where the waters got muddy. She'd said what happened in the stable had been a mistake.

Just after dawn he walked into the kitchen and was thankful it was empty. He needed time. He had to figure everything out. He made some coffee and took it with him to the stable. Then started to work clearing snow on the drives and taking care of livestock. He never stopped. But he kept thinking, and those thoughts went in confusing circles.

He was at Titan's stall when the door to the stable opened, and he didn't have to turn to know Katherine was there. He could sense her presence before he turned and saw he was right. She was just inside the door, taking her hood off and unbuttoning her jacket. She was looking at him, her eyes huge in her face, emphasized by the way she had tugged her hair straight back in a braid. No makeup. No artifice, yet she was lovely, breathtaking.

At that moment the night before made no sense to him. He'd told her so many things, secrets he'd kept to himself for so long, yet in the light of day, he didn't know how to talk to her at all. The pleasure he felt at just seeing her wasn't making anything easier or clearer for him, either. It wasn't his right to feel anything for her, not when she wasn't free.

"Good morning," he said.

"It's almost afternoon."

He hadn't noticed. "No trouble walking down here?"

"No, none." She shrugged. "I think I'm getting used to it...sort of."

"That's something coming from a California girl."

"It snows in California. Just not where I live."

Small talk. Inconsequential talk. It was starting to get on his nerves. Both he and Katherine spoke at the same time.

"Mac?"

"Katherine?"

"Sorry," he said.

"You go first," she said.

He put the pitchfork against the wall, tucking his fingers in the pockets of his jeans. "I meant what I said last night. I've never said those things before. I never wanted to say them out loud." He could see her biting her bottom lip. She looked almost as nervous as he was starting to feel. "And I wanted to say, well, thank you for listening. You do have a gift in getting people to talk, and in the way you listen to them." He forced out words that almost choked him to say. "James is a very lucky man."

That brought high color to her cheeks. "Mac, I—"

The phone rang and he held up one hand. "Hold that thought. I'll be right back."

He hurried into the small office off the hay-storage room and grabbed the phone. "Yes?"

"Parish?"

He knew the voice. He'd only heard it once, but he knew it. "Yes."

"This is James. That lady said she'd put me through to Kate."

It was as though saying the name out loud had brought the call. "Hang on."

He went to give Katherine the phone, feeling as if he'd been kicked in the stomach. James was a fact of her life. A solid fact. He saw her where he'd left her, her impact on him just as great, but now it was tinged with bitterness. "It's for you. It's James."

She only stared at the phone for a moment, then seemed to brace herself before taking it from him. She stood there with it in her hand, not making any effort to put it to her ear. "Aren't you going to talk to him?" he asked.

Her color deepened. "Sure, of course."

She turned from him, halfway facing the door, and finally said, "Hi, James?"

Mac made a point of moving away, grabbing the pitchfork and going back a couple of stalls. But he didn't get back to work. He stabbed the pitchfork into the hay and left it there, then turned, and Katherine was coming toward him, holding the phone out to him.

"Here." Her tone was flat and what color she'd had in her cheeks was gone. "Thanks."

He took it from her. "A problem?"

"I guess you'd call it that."

"You and James?"

"There is no me and James."

Part of him wanted to cheer and the other part

hated to see that look on her face, a look that was somewhere between pain and embarrassment. "If it's anything I've done, I'm sorry. I told you I didn't have much of a conscience before, but even then, I didn't—"

"It's not you. It's me. It's what I've done. What I'm doing."

He moved closer and against his better judgment, touched her cheek. Just one finger. One feather-light touch, but it might as well have been charged with electricity. "What's the old saying about it taking two?"

She looked up at him and stepped away just enough to break his contact with her. "Don't...don't do that," she said in a voice so low he almost missed the words.

"Okay. I know you're upset." He pushed his hands behind his back. "When we get out of here, you tell me where to find James, and I'll tell him the truth." At least the truth that would help her—that it was him, all him. That he'd been the one to reach out to her.

She looked absolutely stricken, and his stomach knotted. "That's not what I'm talking about."

The phone in his hand rang and he answered it, fully expecting it to be James again, wanting to make up. But it was Natty.

"Mackenzie, get up here now. Tyler's had a fall."

He hit the end button, tossed the phone onto a nearby hay bale and started for the door, grabbing his jacket and hat on the way. "Tyler's hurt," he said over his shoulder.

Katherine caught up with him while he was putting on his jacket by the door. "What happened?"

"I don't know," he said, fear alive in him. He put on his hat, then pushed back the door. He set off at a jog, Katherine keeping up, and when he got to the back porch, he took the cleared steps in two strides. He pushed back the door, went inside and called, "Natty!" as he stripped off his jacket and tossed his hat onto the low shelf.

"In here!" she called, and he could hear screaming, too. Tyler. At least he was conscious.

He hurried through the house, all the while aware of Katherine behind him. The little boy's cries echoed down the hallway and led him to the den. He got to the door and found Natty in the middle of the room by the toppled swivel chair, holding Tyler, who was screaming his lungs out. Mac reached for him.

Kate heard the screams and got to the den at the same moment Mac was clearing the desk with a sweep of one hand and putting the screaming Tyler on the bare area. "Get my medical bag," he said to Natty as he checked the boy, feeling his head, looking at his eyes.

"He was after Mr. Boo and he must have climbed on your chair. I heard the crash and found him screaming," she said as she hurried to a closet. Kate stood back and out of the way, watching the two of them with Tyler. Mac checked him out, put a Band-Aid on his forehead, then picked him up and finally the cries started to subside.

"Come on, buddy, you're okay. A small bump on your head, a bit of a scrape. You probably got off easier than Mr. Boo." He looked at Natty over the boy's head, then at Kate. "He's okay. He'll be fine." The cries were gone now and Tyler was leaning into Mac. "We just have to keep him awake for a while to make sure there aren't any complications."

Natty took the boy out of his arms and cuddled him while she looked at Mac. "You're sure he's okay?"

"I'm enough of a doctor to know he'll be fine, just don't let him sleep for a while." He turned to put some things back in his bag. "And keep him calm."

"That's the hard part," Natty said with a relieved smile. "I'll go and get him something to eat. Either one of you want something now? The turkey won't be ready until about six o'clock."

Kate didn't feel at all like eating. First going to the stables to talk with Mac, having James cut in and let her know that he was furious with her when she denied there was any story here, then this. Food was far from what she wanted right then. "No, thank you."

Mac said, "Maybe later."

"Okay," Natty said, and took the boy with her out of the room.

Kate waved to Tyler who was waving bye-bye to her, then she looked back at Mac. She'd lost her chance in the stables, but Mac was here and so was she. All she had to do was close the door the way he had last night, but this time she'd do the talking and the confessing. "Mac?"

"He'll be okay. I may not practice medicine anymore, but I can treat bumps and scrapes.'' He crossed his arms. ''They're child's play.''

He'd been practicing for ten years at least, and he'd been one of the best. ''It's too bad that you don't practice even regular medicine now, that you gave up so much.'' James had told her she'd lost her touch. She'd had the golden goose drop in her lap, he said, and turned it to brass. He was furious. She could deal with that, but Mac had lost everything. She wasn't noble, but whether Mac knew it or not, he was noble. And he was losing because of it. ''You left everything.''

''There wasn't that much to leave,'' he said, his eyes narrowing slightly.

''Do you miss it?''

He eyed her soberly. ''I have my moments.''

''Anything in particular?''

He smiled at that, an endearing, crooked smile that only cemented those new feelings in her. Feelings that were being drowned by her guilt at the moment and the way she was avoiding saying what had to be said. ''Still asking questions, aren't you. I'm here. I'm ranching. I'm keeping a promise.'' The smile was gone. ''And that's it.''

''That's a shame,'' she said without thinking. ''It's a waste. Natty mentioned that the doctor around here, the one at the clinic, Dr....?''

''Peters, Miss Lincoln,'' Mac teased, referring to the story Katherine had told him about her history teacher.

She chuckled at that. ''Okay, Dr. Peters is retiring,

and Natty seems to think you'd be perfect to take over for him.''

''Natty gets crazy ideas. I'm not a GP.''

''No, but you're a good doctor. Maybe you were just doing the wrong sort of doctoring in L.A.''

''I had the wrong life. That included what I did for a living.''

''It wasn't a calling?''

''I guess not.'' His expression was getting darker all the time. ''And that's the end of the questions, okay?''

She bit her lip, ready to face what she had to do, but before she could close the door and say anything, Natty called, ''Mackenzie?''

''What?'' he called back without looking away from Kate.

''Mr. Boo's caught in the drapes again, and Tyler's committing mayhem!''

''Be right there,'' he said, then hesitated before saying, ''I meant what I said. I'll talk to James for you and try to explain.'' He tapped her chin. ''Don't worry. Things will work out one way or the other.''

''Sure,'' she whispered. ''One way or the other.''

Chapter Thirteen

It was Kate's first real Thanksgiving, sitting around a table laden with food, with Tyler, Natty and Mac. It gave her a glimpse of what a family could be, and for that moment she was thankful she hadn't had the chance to confess to Mac. She wouldn't have had this time with the three of them. A memory to tuck away, she thought, to recall when she was feeling lonely. She was good at keeping memories, but most of them had been make-believe, the way she wished her life had been when she was a child.

"This was a phenomenal meal," Kate said to Natty as she pushed her plate away.

"It's just plain old cooking," Natty said, waving off the compliment.

"Maybe to you, but to me this is great. The closest I've ever had to a real holiday meal before was a frozen turkey dinner."

"Well, when you're single and live alone, you tend to rely on frozen dinners."

She felt her cheeks heat up a bit. "A frozen dinner was my mother's idea of a big dinner."

"Not around here. The bigger the meal the better.'' She looked at Mac. ''You done?'' she asked him.

He'd eaten only half of what he had on his plate and had been nursing a cup of coffee for a while. ''Done.''

''Well, keep down the praise,'' Natty said, and got up to go around to Tyler's chair and take him out of it.

''It was good,'' Mac murmured, and looked down into his coffee cup.

''Great praise indeed,'' Natty said as she set the boy on the floor and watched him take off. ''Be still my heart.''

Kate smiled. She really liked Natty. She liked her way of dealing with Mac, and she liked her love for a family that wasn't really hers. That sobered Kate. Loving someone who wasn't hers, who wouldn't be hers. As soon as Mac knew the truth, this would probably stop dead.

She felt as if the warm air in the room was growing thinner all the time, and she stood, picked up her dishes crossed to the sink. ''Just show me where the detergent is and I'll get the dishes started.''

''Bless you, child,'' Natty said with a grin. ''Offer for help with the dishes.'' She looked at Mac. ''Extremely rare occurrence around here.''

He picked up his dishes, brought them over to the sink and handed them to Kate. ''I can't take this abuse,'' he said with a smile at Natty, then looked at Kate and the smile faltered. ''I'll check things in the barn, then be back up.''

She took his dishes from him and he was gone

before she had the plate rinsed. She and Natty worked to clean up the evidence of the huge meal, then Tyler trotted back into the room, tugging a small wagon filled with blocks. He settled by the door to the hallway and played while they put away the extra food and finished up.

Natty turned to Kate when the last dish was done, wiped her hands and said, "What a good day."

"Yes," Kate said softly, wiping her hands, then putting the towel on a side rack. "It *has* been good." What an understatement.

Natty exhaled. "I'm tired, ready for bed," she said as the back door opened, then closed. Mac had returned, bringing the cool night air with him into the room.

"Good timing," Natty said. "We're finished."

"I work on it."

"You've perfected it," Natty said, barely covering a yawn.

"Do you want me to keep an eye on Tyler while you get ready for bed?" Kate asked.

"Now that's a change. I don't have to bribe you anymore."

"No, I guess you don't," Kate said, and knew that she was as precariously close to loving the child as much as she loved the man. She glanced at Mac and found him watching her, a smile touching his lips. She wished she could smile back at him, but it was too painful. She suddenly felt totally overwhelmed, and tears threatened to surface. "I…I need to take care of something, then I'll come back and watch him," she said, and hurried out of the kitchen into the short hallway.

As she went toward her room, she saw the door was ajar; she was certain she'd closed it earlier. Then her heart leaped to her throat. Tyler had been at the door to the kitchen playing blocks. She hadn't even noticed he wasn't there when she passed by. She'd been so involved in her own thoughts and getting away for a minute. Her purse was out, and the pepper spray was in it.

She hurried to the door, went into the room and stopped dead. Tyler was in there, all right, but he wasn't doing anything. He was on the bed, curled up on his side, sleeping, and her purse was still safely closed on the nightstand. Her first reaction was total relief, then total panic when she remembered Mac saying he shouldn't sleep. Fear ripped through her and she yelled, "Mac! Mac!" as she rushed to the bed.

She barely reached Tyler before he opened his eyes and let out his own screams. By the time Mac got there with Natty on his heels, Kate was trying to pick the boy up, but he was fighting her tooth and nail. Mac reached in, caught Tyler and drew him into his arms. "What's wrong?" he asked, looking over the boy at Kate.

"He…he was sleeping," she said, only aware then that she was crying. "And you said he shouldn't and I thought…" She stopped on a gulp. "Oh, God," she breathed.

Mac was staring at her as if she'd lost her mind, holding the boy who was obviously just fine. "It's okay," he said as Natty reached for Tyler. "I just meant for an hour or two after the fall."

"Oh, shoot," she muttered, swiping at her tears.

"Katherine, you didn't know."

She didn't know so much! She sniffed and swiped at her tears again. "Damn it, I thought…" Her heart was still hammering in her chest, and that fear… She looked at the boy. Oh, yes, she loved him. She loved him so much that she'd scared everyone. "I'm sorry."

"An honest mistake," Mac said. "A very honest mistake."

That made her feel even worse. She wasn't honest. She hadn't been from the first moment they'd met. "Sure," she muttered.

"I think I'll take him up to bed now, and I'll get myself to sleep," Natty said.

"I was going to watch him for you," Kate said, and knew that the last thing Natty probably wanted at that point was a half-crazed woman watching the boy.

"Thanks, but I can manage. I'll put him to bed first."

Kate looked at her, then at the boy. "Night, Tyler," she said softly.

He cocked his head to one side and smiled at her, a dimpled expression that belied her scaring him just moments ago. "Nigh', Nigh'," he mumbled.

Natty started to the door with him, then turned back to Kate. "Maybe you should lock your door so he can't get in here again."

"I will," she said, and Natty was gone.

Mac studied Kate. "Are you okay?"

"It seems you're always asking me that, doesn't it?"

He smiled wryly. "That seems to be my habit."

"You know, I haven't been sick a day in my life. I can't remember the last time I went to a doctor, and heaven knows, I've never fainted. And getting crazy... Shoot. Then mucking stables, trudging through the snow, being with a two-year-old." She shrugged, a fluttery motion. "A first for everything."

Her own words struck her hard. A first for so much, and it all centered on Mac. Especially the part about falling in love. God knew she'd never done that before. But she loved Mac. She could barely breathe and looked down at her clutched hands.

"A lot of firsts," he said softly.

"Live and learn," she said, then made herself look back up at him. She was too tired even to think of how to start telling him the truth now. "I'm beat."

He stood there quietly, and when he finally spoke, he said, "Tomorrow the roads should be cleared. You'll be leaving?"

It made her middle tighten to hear him say the words. "I guess so."

"Once Carl gets your car going, are you heading to Shadow Ridge?"

She couldn't focus. "I don't think so."

"The offer's still good," he said.

"What offer?"

"To talk to James, to explain. I meant it when I offered it. I don't want to mess things up for you."

She'd done a good enough job messing things up

for herself. "No, no," she murmured. "Don't worry about it."

He was at the door, opening it, turning the lock to make sure it worked. He hesitated, looking at her. "We'll call Carl in the morning and figure things out."

She was sure Carl couldn't figure out anything about her, but she nodded, angry that the tears were threatening to come back. She didn't want to feel like this. She didn't want to feel confused and afraid. "Mac?" Tears. She could feel them on her cheeks, but couldn't stop them. "Shoot!"

He was close, bending over her, touching her, his hand warm on her cheek. "What is it?"

She tried to say, "Nothing." She tried to stop the tears, but she couldn't. A thought had come to her, and it possessed her now. She didn't want him to hate her, and he would when he knew what a liar she was. She couldn't bear that on top of everything else. One look at him and things seemed so simple. Just stop. Just walk away and never say a thing.

James thought there was no story. She'd make sure he believed it. Then she'd figure out what to do with her life. Whatever that life would be. At the moment she knew that her life had to be without Mac and everything she'd discovered in the past few days. That would be gone. But he wouldn't be hurt anymore. The story wouldn't see the light of day. And he wouldn't hate her. She needed a miracle to pull this off. A miracle on par with her finding that love came at the oddest, most inopportune times in this life. And that it all hung on such a frail thing as the human heart.

"Katherine?" he whispered as he came back, closing the door behind him.

She wanted to just say, "You know, I love you," but that was suicide. "Cabin fever," she managed to say. "It's making me weird."

He laughed, a soft, rich sound that filtered through the chill her lies had drawn around her. "Sorry, you can't blame cabin fever for making you weird."

"Great," she muttered.

"You've been through a lot."

She'd never been through this—loving someone and seeing that someone slip away. And not being able to do anything about it. "But I...I never cry," she said on a sniffle.

"Another first?" he whispered.

She closed her eyes. "Oh, Mac, I never..."

"I never have, either," he whispered, and went closer to her. "Never wanted someone so much."

Kate looked up at him, his image blurred slightly by the tears, and a sense of desperation filled her. She'd fashioned memories for herself ever since she was a child. Making some up out of whole cloth, and some she'd embellished and some she took at face value. She touched his face, felt his reality under her fingertips and knew that this memory would be real. Completely real. And it would have to last a lifetime.

She moved closer, lifted her face his and whispered, "But I want to." She knew making love would change everything, but it was a risk she was willing to take.

He never said a thing before he found her lips. And she opened her mouth to his, welcoming his invasion, desperate to taste him and start the memories building. The roughness of his new beard on her skin, the incredible softness of his lips, the way his fingers tangled in her hair, the way each breath he took seemed to draw her breath out and mingle with hers.

She wrapped her arms around him, yearning toward him, that need she'd felt every time he got close, threatening to consume her. The need was raw and almost painful. And she knew that nothing would stop it except being with Mac completely. She needed skin against skin, heart against heart, and she tugged at his shirt, desperate to make that contact. Her hands felt awkward, her fingers unresponsive, and Mac was the one who moved back enough to strip off his shirt, then he touched the buttons on her shirt.

Without looking away from her, he undid each one, then eased off her shirt and tossed it somewhere behind him. She faced him, the lace of her bra the only barrier left, and as he slowly moved the bra straps off her shoulders. She literally held her breath, trembling when his hands moved to her back and undid the fastener.

Then lace was gone, and Mac stood inches from her. His gaze dropped to her breasts and without his even touching her, her nipples responded, hardening to nubs, and the ache in her grew heavier and more urgent. "Oh, my God," he whispered, then touched her, and she gasped when his hands cupped her breasts. Her legs were weak, her breathing rapid, and she swayed toward him.

She tumbled into his arms and felt as if she'd finally come home. As though she'd been lost and he'd found her. Yet she'd never been here before. She lifted her face to his and the kiss was immediate and burning. It seared into her soul, drawing at her being, and she felt as if she was whole for the first time in her life. That the other part of her soul had been lost was back.

She was lifted in his arms, then together they were on the bed, tangled in the comforter, legs and arms twined, blurring the start of one and the ending of the other. Mac's hands were everywhere, touching, caressing, drawing feeling from her, building pleasures in her that soared. Her jeans were gone and she didn't know how, and Mac's hand was on her stomach, his fingers under the band of her panties.

She lifted her hips, letting him slip the flimsy material off her, and he found her center. His hand pressed against her, and she moved against him, sensations shooting through her, knotting in her middle and threatening to explode. He entered her, one finger, then two, and she rose up and back, instinctively pressing into his touch, needing it more and more.

Then suddenly he was gone. She opened her eyes and he was above her. In a moment he had his jeans off, the white of his briefs stark against his tanned skin. The cotton barely contained his desire, and then the cotton was gone. She found him and circled him, startled that touching him and holding him seemed as natural as each breath she took. Hearing him groan roughly only made her more certain that this memory was just hers. That for this one moment in time, Mac was hers, and she wanted to be his.

He moved his legs between hers, and she felt his silken strength against her, heard him whisper her name. Slowly he entered her until he filled her. She lifted her hips and he gasped, then he initiated the first stroke. Deep and sure, then again and again, and she matched him, thrust for thrust.

The sensations grew with blinding speed, higher and higher, freeing her in a way she'd never thought possible. Claiming every atom of her being, pushing away everything else but herself and Mac. A fantasy that for this moment in time was real. It was her reality. Greater than any reality she'd ever known. And as she soared higher and higher, she arched upward, willing herself to let go completely. To give everything, one time. This time. With Mac.

And she did. There was nothing she held back, nothing denied when the world around her exploded, when she heard Mac say her name from a great distance, when she heard a sob. Her sob. Her tears. Her love. And she held on to Mac, afraid to let go, afraid to come back to earth. Afraid to face the loss she knew would be hers when the fantasy was gone.

The fear grew as fast as the glory faded. Then she was in Mac's arms, lying with him, his arms around her, and she closed her eyes tightly. She'd make this last, at least for a bit longer. She'd make this last for this night. One night. Her night. She pressed a kiss to Mac's chest, tasting the saltiness of his damp skin, then put her cheek against his heart. She listened to each beat, steady, sure, strong, and it was the last thing she heard before drifting off to sleep.

MAC WOKE from a deep, wonderful sleep to soft darkness and Katherine by his side. Surrounded by her heat, with the sense of completeness in him, he held on to that feeling. He felt each breath she took, her heart beating against his side, her hand lying on his chest. It struck him right then that finding Katherine had brought him something he hadn't had for most of his life. Peace.

He exhaled. Peace. God, it felt like a balm to his soul. And it was all because of Katherine. One woman with green eyes and a way of touching him that gave him life. It was so simple, yet so remarkable.

His heart lurched when she sighed softly, then settled again, and the idea that despite a past filled with many women, she was the first who could make him smile just coming into a room, who could make him feel lonelier than he ever thought possible when she left that room. The first woman who looked as lovely mucking out a stall as she did lying in the hay with him. The first to touch him on so many levels that he couldn't even name all of them.

The first who made him want and need a connection that he'd always thought he could, and would, live without. And the first who made him see the foolishness in his belief for thirty-five years that love was for the few, and not for him. Love? She exhaled softly and he felt a sense of coming home that rocked him. Katherine? A woman he hadn't even known existed a few days ago had become the center of his being. Yes, the first to touch his soul.

He pressed a kiss to her silky hair, and he felt her stir in his embrace.

"You awake?" she asked in a whisper through the darkness around them.

"I didn't think you were." He felt her shift, then her hand was stroking lazy circles on his chest, and the contact was starting to draw at him, starting to bring back a need for her that he thought he'd just satisfied.

"Barely," she said on a sigh.

How could he tell her that he didn't want to sleep, that he didn't want to lose a moment with her? It sounded so corny to say, "I want to feel you and look at you and never take my eyes off you." So, instead, he said, "I've been thinking about things, and I wanted to ask you something."

She shifted, moving slightly from him to raise herself on elbow and look down at him. Shadows blurred and robbed him of the details of her face, but they couldn't take away the tension her breath brushing his bare skin built in him. "What?" she asked.

He touched her cheek with the tips of his fingers, the connection vital and compelling. "You…can you stay a while?"

He felt her exhale a shaky breath. "Stay?"

He slipped his hand to the nape of her neck and laced his fingers in her tangled hair. "Stay. Here." Two words, and they were the first time he'd ever asked any woman to stay with him. There was no walking away from Katherine. He knew that he never wanted to walk away from her. "Stay with me?"

She was silent for so long he started to feel fear. What would happen if she said no and left. Would he cease to exist? Would what happened in those months after Mike died, that sense of not being connected in this world at all, return? He pulled her gently down to him, found her lips, kissing her with as much need as passion, then eased her back when he felt she wasn't responding to him.

Maybe if she didn't speak, if she didn't answer, it wouldn't end. Maybe he could will this not to end. He kissed her again to keep her words at bay, to keep any mention of anyone else out of the space around them. He trailed his touch along her cheek, and he tasted the saltiness of tears. That stopped him and he drew back. He couldn't hurt her, not in any way. "I'm sorry," he breathed.

"No, no, no," she whispered unsteadily. "Don't be. Please. I can't…"

No, he didn't want that. He didn't want rejection. He just wanted her. Forever. "Forget what I said. Just forget it, and we'll talk in the morning, okay?"

She took a shuddering breath, then murmured, "Yes…in the morning…" Then she was there, she was the one kissing him with an urgency that was almost painful.

And he could forget for a while as she touched him, stroked him, found his almost instant response to her. He gasped as she circled his desire and arched toward the contact. There was no hesitation, no cautiousness in her. She was there, her kisses on him, stroking him, almost frantically, drawing at his soul.

He wanted her, he wanted to be in her, and when she hesitated, he hesitated. He didn't want her to stop. She didn't. She shifted to get over him, to straddle his hips, then as his hands spanned her waist, she eased herself down on him until he filled her. And everything stopped. She was connected to him, her hair a shadowy veil around her face, and each breath she took echoed his own. Not moving. Neither one of them. Her hands were braced on his shoulders, and he had a sense of her totally surrounding him, absorbing him.

After what could have been a second or an eternity, she exhaled on a shuddering breath. Then she moved, slowly at first, and every fear he'd had moments ago was pushed away by a fiery passion that threatened to consume him. Exquisite sensations of filling her thrilled him, and hearing her moan softly with each stroke, only stoked the fires in him.

He wanted this forever, wanted it to never stop, then he heard her gasp, and completeness came in one stunning moment of feeling. He heard his own voice whispering her name over and over again, and her soft moans filling his ears. He never wanted to leave her. She was the reason he was alive. The reason he was here. Katherine. The reason for everything.

They rolled onto their sides, still holding each other. He felt her get as close as was humanly possible and he held her even tighter. Tomorrow they'd talk. He'd be able to think of the words that would make her stay with him forever.

MAC NEVER SLEPT for more than a few hours at time, but when he finally awoke, the dawn was there, cold, crisp light filtering through the frosted windowpanes. Katherine was still sleeping, against his side. She'd turned away from him sometime during the night, so her back was against his front, their legs tangled together. He had an arm around her waist and could feel her heart beating in unison with his.

He lay there absorbing the feeling of not being alone, of her being part of him. And she slept. He could have stayed there forever, but he realized that he had things to do before he asked her if she'd stay, at least for a while. He'd call Carl, find out about the chains and about the roads, then if they were clear, he'd go and take care of everything for her.

He kissed her lightly on the cheek and she stirred softly, then resettled, her hands folded under her cheeks the way a child slept. "I'll be back," he whispered softly, then eased away and out of bed. The cold was instant and jarring, and it took all of his strength to turn away from her and get dressed. He saw her purse on the nightstand and reached for it. Her keys were in a side pocket, and he took them, then with one last look at her, he left the room.

Chapter Fourteen

Natty was in the kitchen with Tyler when Mac went through to get his things and go to the truck. "Heard anything about the roads?" he asked as he ducked into the mudroom and got his jacket, boots and hat.

"Cleared out to the Jessop place. Just talked to Arlene. The plows are there now. And they cleared out front. I thought you'd hear the noise. It about woke the dead. It sure as heck woke him." She motioned to Tyler, but never looked away from Mac. "You slept well?"

She wasn't going to say anything directly, but she was digging. He didn't have time to sidestep her questions, so he just shrugged and said, "Can I have a cup of coffee to take with me? I'm heading into town to see about Katherine's car."

She turned and poured a mug of coffee for him. As she brought it to him, she said, "Is she leaving today?"

He took the mug. "I don't know. Tell her I'll back as soon as I can when she gets up?"

"Of course."

"Good." With that, he went back through the

mudroom and out into the cold crisp new day. He got the truck from the barn and headed into to town. Carl was in his shop, despite the early hour, and looked up as Mac came inside. "Morning to you. Up early, aren't you?"

"I came to see about the lady's car chains. Did you have any luck with them?"

"So, she sat out the storm at your place?"

"Yeah, and I came to see about the chains."

"Got them right here," Carl said. "They got here not more than ten minutes ago." He patted a large box on the counter.

"I'll go with you to get the car, and I'll drive it back."

Carl nodded, then called over his shoulder, "Davy, watch the shop. I'm taking the tow truck down the road."

The disembodied voice of Carl's kid brother called back from the storeroom, "Sure thing."

Carl got his jacket, and he and Mac took the tow truck back to find Katherine's car. They nearly missed it because the snow had swallowed it, making it little more than a large mound on the side of the road. Within minutes, Carl and Mac had dug out the rear of the car enough to get the tow chain attached to the bumper, then slowly pulled it up and onto the road.

After clearing the windows of snow, Mac opened the driver's-side door and slipped inside. Remarkably, the engine started right up, and he left it idling while he and Carl put the chains on the wheels.

"I'll follow you back to your place," Mac said.

"You can follow me in my truck out to the ranch, then I'll drive you back."

"You got it," Carl said, and climbed back in the tow truck.

Mac felt like a little kid on Christmas Day, so anxious to get back to Katherine he could barely stand it. He got behind the wheel, reached to adjust the seat for his legs, then went to toss his hat on the passenger seat. He stopped when he noticed a folder lying on the seat and his name on it in huge block letters running down the right side. Just then Carl honked at him as the truck pulled up beside the compact car.

Mac gave him a thumbs-up, and Carl took off. Mac laid his hat on the dash and stared at the folder, at a colored logo in the top right-hand corner, a logo he'd seen before. A magazine of some sort, not a tabloid, but a "celebrity" type of magazine. And his name, Dr. Mackenzie Parish, under the logo.

KATE AWOKE to someone whispering, "Kay, Kay, Kay, Kay," over and over again and something tickling her nose. A dream that kept going, or … Mac? She remembered the fantasy, those moments when nothing mattered except being with him. She opened her eyes, wanting to see just Mac, to memorize his face again, to make sure she never forgot. No matter what happened.

She opened her eyes, but Mac wasn't there. Tyler, so close to her face that he was almost blurry, was brushing a little stuffed animal at her face. Now he stood back, grinned at her, dropped the toy and poked her arm with a finger. ''Kay, up!''

''Kay?'' she asked as she tugged the sheets higher. She was quite naked under them. ''What're you doing here, buddy?'' she asked, looking past him to see if Mac was there.

''Come, box,'' he said.

''Blocks?''

''Uh-uh,'' he said, emphatically nodding his head.

''Okay, okay,'' she said, needing to see Mac. ''Where's Daddy?''

''Daddy all gone.''

''Gone?''

''To get your car,'' Natty said as she came into the room and scooped the little boy up in her arms. ''He'll be back soon. Said to tell you so. I thought you were going to lock your door and keep this guy out?''

''I thought Mac did,'' she said.

''So, did you have a good night?'' she asked.

Kate knew her face was coloring, and wondered how much Natty knew about what had happened. ''Fine, thanks.''

''I think everyone did,'' Natty murmured, not coming out and saying anything directly. Thank goodness. ''Why don't you get dressed, and I'll start some cocoa.''

''That sounds good,'' Kate said. ''By the way, when did Mac leave?''

''A while ago.'' Natty hesitated. ''The roads are clear and … Are you leaving today?''

Kate nodded. ''If my car's working.''

"Should be," Natty said, then added, "Get dressed and come on out so we can talk a bit while we have the chance before Mackenzie gets back."

"I'll be right there," Kate said, and Natty took Tyler out with her, then closed the door on his cries for, "Box, box!"

She took a breath, bracing herself for whatever happened. She knew she couldn't just leave. Sneaking out of town wasn't possible. She'd known that sometime during the night, sometime when Mac had touched her. No more lies. There couldn't be more lies, even if she never saw him again.

But after making love with Mac, she'd begun to hope that he could forgive her. That if she reassured him she'd never write anything about him, that he could at least not hate her. After last night, she had hope. Something she rarely felt in her life. And it felt good.

"WHAT THE HELL?" Mac grabbed the folder while Katherine's car idled.

The heater was starting to work, but the chill in him deepened as he lifted the folder and read a list of handwritten names under his own. A name per line, then notations in the next column. Research, fact find, search. And dates to the right. The entries started about two years before he left Los Angeles. He skimmed them, twenty or more, and stopped at the last two and most recent entries. The first was dated about six days ago, signed by James Lowe with no reason given for the entry. Then the last one was dated the day before he found Katherine stranded in the snow.

The signature on that one was Kate Ames done, and the reason given was "assignment research."

Nausea welled up in him, all the excitement he'd felt moments ago gone as if it had never been. He opened the folder and found the old Mac Parish. Pictures and articles and notes on the "doctor to the stars." The logo was for the monthly gossip magazine the *Final Word*. It was stamped everywhere.

A reporter. A story. He tossed the file onto the seat, his pain so acute he was afraid he couldn't keep breathing. But he not only kept breathing, he drove the small car into the town, then followed his own truck with Carl driving back to the ranch. Carl parked the truck by the front of the house, and Mac stopped Katherine's car behind it. He got out, called to Carl that he'd be right out, then headed into the house.

He went through the living room gripping the keys to Katherine's car so tightly they almost cut into his palm. Then he saw her coming out of the bedroom, and despite everything, just the sight of her made him ache. But now that ache didn't come from need— although it shocked him that he could still want her—but from knowing he never had what he thought he'd had. Never. It was all a lie. She was a lie. And even though he'd never really had her, his anger at what she'd stolen from him was unbearable.

WHEN KATE SAW the look on Mac's face, the smile on her face disappeared in an instant. He came to her without a word and caught her by her upper arm.

Before she could think of what to say or do, he pulled her back into her room and closed the door behind them.

He let her go, and she looked up, stunned at the change in the face of the man who had made love to her during the night. Now his eyes were cold, his expression tight. She could hear his breathing, saw the way he pulled his hands back and pushed them into the pockets of his jacket.

"We're going to talk right now, right here," he said, his voice barely above a whisper, low and rough. "And Natty isn't to know anything about this. Agreed?"

She didn't even know what she was agreeing to, but she nodded. "Sure, yes, okay," she said and would have reached out to make some contact with him, any contact, but his words stopped her dead.

"I thought I'd spilled enough to you to make a damn good story, but I guess you thought if you slept with me I'd tell you even more."

"What?"

"Spill my guts, confess to God knows what. That's what you were looking for, wasn't it? That angle on your story, more shocking details of the 'doctor to the stars?' That lurid twist that would make your exclusive perfect and up the circulation?"

Her heart sank. He knew. She didn't how or when, but he knew, and her worst fear was realized. There was no forgiveness, no understanding, but very real hatred. That hatred was every bit as strong as their passion of the night before. "Can I explain?"

He uttered a profanity that rocked her, then ground out, "Forget it. I don't need to hear more lies."

"No, the truth. I'll tell you—"

"Stop. There's no point in talking after all," he said, his anger fading, but leaving nothing in its wake. He was shutting down completely. No hatred, no anger, just nothing. And his words dropped to a flatness that was almost as painful to hear as the anger had been moments before. He was leaving her, not physically, not yet, but emotionally. He was gone. And she was very much alone. That terrified her.

"Mac, please—"

"No." The single word was flat, but jarred her all the way to her soul. He didn't want to hear anything she had to say.

Whatever she'd thought had happened between them was just her reactions, her needs, her love. She felt the cold then, a harsh, cutting coldness that seemed to gather around her. "I'm so sorry," she said, and she was…all too late.

"Get out."

"I…I'll leave," she managed to say.

"Good. But if you even think of doing a story about me, I'll sue everyone. If I ever see anything I told you about me in print, or anything about Mike or Tyler, I'll do whatever it takes to stop you. I'll take you and your damn James and the whole magazine down. Do you understand?"

She tried to say she'd never write that story, that she never could have, but before she could do more than nod, he pulled his hand out of his pocket and held out something toward her. Keys. Her keys, and he was holding them as if they were a poisonous snake, between his thumb and forefinger.

"Your car's outside. Get in it and get out of here. I'll tell Natty that you couldn't wait to make a break for it, that James is pining for you, that you're on a mission to get to him. I'll tell her whatever I can think of. You just go, and make it fast." Before she could put her hand out to take the keys, he let them drop to the floor between them, then spun on his heel and left.

He closed the door carefully, no slam, no jarring action. It was just shut, and she was alone. "I'm sorry," she whispered to the closed door. "I'm so sorry."

She'd let herself hope. She'd let herself believe that the truth would make things right. How stupid she'd been. She picked up the keys, shocked that the metal held heat, Mac's heat, and she closed her hand around them. That was all she had left, and that, too, would be gone in moments.

The door opened and the hope that Mac had come back was dashed when Natty stood there. "Mackenzie said you had to leave right away." The woman looked troubled, but Kate doubted Mac had said anything. He'd told her that Natty wasn't to know about her. "Is it true?"

"Yes…I…" She had to turn from Natty, making herself cross the room to retrieve. "I need to get going, and Mac got my car, and…" She bit her lip hard as she picked up her purse and pushed her keys in it, then closed her eyes. "Thank you for everything."

She jumped when Natty touched her arm. "Honey, you don't have to go."

Kate didn't want this. She didn't want the woman to be so kind. "I do."

"Mackenzie hasn't had it easy, you know." She let go of Kate, but Kate didn't turn to her as she continued speaking. "He's been so lost and so sad. I've been worried sick about him. But these last few days, he's...." Kate heard the woman sigh heavily. "He's started to act as if he's alive again. I know it's because of you."

Kate turned then, tears stinging her eyes. "I'm sorry." She swallowed hard and the tears slipped down her cheeks. She went around Natty to where her jacket lay across the side chair. Quickly she put it on. "I'm so sorry, but I have to go."

Natty didn't try to argue anymore, but said softly, "You can always come back."

"No, I don't think so." Kate clutched the purse tightly, then turned, not bothering to brush at her tears. There was no point when so many more were waiting to fall. "But thank you so much for...for being here. I don't know what I would have done..." She bit her lip hard. "Thank you."

Natty moved to her and hugged her. For a moment Kate clung to her. It would be so easy, like holding to a mother who could make things right. But things couldn't be right. They wouldn't be right, and Natty would probably hate her as much as Mac did if she knew why she'd come here. "You call, okay?" Natty said as she stood back.

"Sure," Kate said, and knew it was her last lie in this house. She wouldn't be calling.

"Come and say goodbye to Tyler?"

Kate didn't think she could endure that. "Can you tell him I had to go?"

"I could." Natty looked hard at Kate. "Okay, I will. He'll miss you."

"I'll miss him," Kate admitted, surprising herself that she'd ever say that about a child or that she could love a child. She'd never see him again, either. "I'll miss you."

"That's it?" Natty asked.

No, it wasn't. But she had no choice. "That's it."

Natty crossed to the door, paused, looked back at Kate as if she wanted to say something else. Then she left, closing the door quietly behind her. Kate was alone. Completely alone.

She took one last look around the room, then slipped out into the hallway and flinched when she heard Tyler laughing in the kitchen. She went in the other direction, out the front door and to her car, idling in the driveway. She climbed in and saw the file on the front seat, the papers askew. She'd forgotten all about it. Obviously Mac had found it.

Before leaving she took out her cell phone, saw that she had a signal, and pushed in a number. When James answered, she braced herself and closed her eyes as she did the last thing she could do for Mac and the people he loved.

"HELL'S BELLS," Carl muttered when Mac told him about Kate. "They've been around before, asking questions, trying to bribe people, but I thought they'd lost interest. And who would have thought that someone like her would be a snake from the press?"

Snake from the press? Mac stopped the truck in front of Carl's shop. He hadn't told Carl any of the personal horror—that was over and done. That was his burden to bear. "Yeah, who would have thought?" he muttered, and got out.

He followed Carl into the shop, and Dave looked up from sorting lug nuts on the counter. "Can I get going now?" Dave asked Carl.

"Sure, no problem," Carl said, and the boy was gone before Carl finished the sentence. Then he looked at Mac. "So, you put the fear of God into her?"

"I hope so," he replied, suddenly realizing he had no place go until Katherine cleared off the ranch.

"What about that boss of hers, or boyfriend, or whatever the hell that guy James is? What's she told him?"

He should have thought about that. But all he'd been able to think about was Katherine and what she'd done. "Damn it, you're right. He's the one who'll run the story." He motioned to Carl's phone. "Can I use it?"

"Sure." Carl pushed it across the counter to him. "Help yourself."

Mac called information, got the number for the magazine, put it through, then went through a maze of operators to finally get to James Lowe's extension. A man answered. "Features, Lowe."

"Lowe, this is Mac Parish."

There was stunned silence for a long moment, then the man said, "Dr. Parish?"

"Shut up and listen. If you run any story on me, it had better be about me disappearing and you having no idea why. Under no circumstances are you to run anything that Katherine Ames gives you. If you do, you'll regret it. I'll ruin you and the magazine."

There was a low whistle, then James said, "So, there *is* a story there. She told me there wasn't, that you were a dead end, a bum on a ranch, and that was that. But I thought there was something else. Something that would make her quit like that and take off on her own. What in hell happened out there? What did you do to her?"

Mac closed his eyes tightly. "What are you talking about?"

"Kate quit. She left the magazine. She's not coming back." He laughed, a strange sound that held no humor. "Can you believe that after all I've done for her? This woman has the ability to make a stone talk to her, and she's walking away. She'll starve out in the real world. Or maybe she'll write some damn novel like she wanted to when she was a kid. She left here focused and somewhere along the line, she got lost."

Mac understand that all too well. "She quit?"

"She said she'd had it. That there was no story. That you were a bore, and I'd do well to leave you alone."

She wasn't going to do a story. "Take her advice," Mac said. "Leave me and my family alone."

"You know what, Doc? You aren't worth this. I lost my best features writer, and any has-been doctor isn't worth the paper to write the story on. There won't be a story on you."

"That's all I wanted to know," Mac said.

"Oh, Doc, before you hang up? Would you do me a favor? When you see Kate, tell her I'll always take her back?"

Mac hung up without answering. When he saw Katherine? He'd done some stupid things in his life. He'd made messes of unbelievable proportions, and he'd just done it again. He'd thrown away the only thing he'd ever found in this world that made life worth living. He called the ranch. "Natty, is she there?" he asked without any preamble.

"She'd gone, Mackenzie."

"When?"

"Fifteen minutes ago. She was crying. Mackenzie, I—"

"We'll talk later," he said, and hung up. "Carl, if she stops by, keep her here any way you can and call me."

"What?" the man asked, shock on his face. "What's up now?"

"Just make her stay here, no matter what, and call me," he repeated as he started for the door.

"Sure, Kenny," he called as Mac left.

The brightness of the snowy world was everywhere, and it took Mac a minute to adjust his eyes from the dimness in the shop. He'd driven her away the same way he had Mike. For all the wrong reasons. Because he wouldn't listen. Because he couldn't get past what was happening with himself. He looked up the street, and as if by a miracle, she was there. Her rental car was coming down the freshly plowed street.

"Katherine?" he shouted. "Katherine!" He waved, running toward the street, but she kept going. He turned and ran for his truck.

KATE COULD BARELY SEE because of the glare bouncing off the snow. Her eyes were dry now. It was over, everything was over. She passed through the small town of Bliss, looking straight ahead, and she felt so empty. Everything was gone. She'd resigned from her job when she talked to James and had no idea how she'd support herself. There was no job. No bonus. No Mac. No future. Just her. She'd never felt more alone in her life.

She passed the last of the stores where the plows had piled mounds of snow on either side of the street. The heater in the car was working, but she was shaking and couldn't stop. She'd learned as a very young child not to beg, to take what happened to her and get used to it. She'd learned to get on with things and not dwell on anything for more than a few minutes. Her parents had taught her well to push all her feelings deep down inside and get on with life.

But this time she was failing miserably.

How could she push the past few days down and not remember? How could she not remember how it felt to have hope? She would always remember. She

was on the main road now, cleared to two narrow
lanes, banked high with snow on either side. She'd
drive back to the airport, return to Los Angeles and
figure out what to do from there.

Kate rounded a curve and saw a sign barely clearing the piled snow. "Leaving Bliss. Come on back."

Oddly, after all the pain and sorrow that filled her,
the sign was the last straw. Tears slid silently down
her cheeks again, burning hot and aching. Then it
wasn't just tears. It was sobs, strange noises that almost sounded like hiccups, shaking her body. She
wiped at her eyes, kept going, then off to the left she
saw a spot that had to be where her car had spent
most of the past week.

The snow was scattered, deep tire paths going
from a low spot to the main road, and footprints
pressed into the snow. Deep holes in the whiteness.
Her tears increased. She looked away from the spot
at the same time she felt the back of the car start to
skid. Déjà vu, the same as the night she'd met Mac,
the loss of control.

But this time it wasn't storming, it wasn't night,
and she didn't get to park on the side of the road.
She braked, and that only made the car go faster
downhill, veering off to the right into the deep drifts
of snow, through them, tipping into a gully, going
toward snow-laden pines.

She screamed as she pressed the brakes and tried
frantically to steer away from the massive trees and
stop the downward plunge. But nothing worked, and
she hurled forward and down, jarring, sliding, then
she saw one tree dead ahead. And it stopped the car.

A jarring, bone-shaking, sickening impact that despite the seat belt restraint, sent her forward, lurching her back, spreading pain through her head and neck, across her chest, then overwhelming sickness all through her.

As the world came to a standstill, the pain grew and all Kate could think was that she was dying and there was no going back, no way to take back the things she'd done to Mac. No way to make up for what she'd done. And in the end, she was alone. Completely alone.

A horn sounded, darkness was there, soft sinking, and for a second she thought she heard Mac calling her over the raucous horn. Then everything was black.

Chapter Fifteen

Mac drove as fast as he could after Katherine down the winding road bordered by high piles of plowed snow on either side. He rounded a curve, felt the truck slip slightly, then get traction, just as he spotted the pathway gouged in the snow to the right.

It was wide enough for a small car to go through. He slowed as he neared the opening. The sound of a horn cut through the air. He stopped, climbed out of his truck and again heard the horn blare into the frigid air. He climbed through the bank of snow to the edge of the gully beyond, the sound getting louder and louder, then he saw the car. Nose-down, its progress apparently stopped by a massive pine. The engine was still idling, the exhaust curling into the cold air. Katherine's car.

He'd heard of fear making people focused and centered. Right then his whole focus was on reaching Katherine. He started down the side of the gully, slipping and sliding. He'd never been one to pray, but all the way down he said a simple prayer over and over again: "Let her be okay. Let her be okay."

Then he was by the driver's door. He saw Katherine behind the wheel, slumped awkwardly to her right, her hand pressed to the horn, blood trickling down her cheek. Her eyes were closed and she wasn't moving.

"Katherine!" he screamed as he grabbed the door handle and pulled, but it wouldn't give. It was either locked or jammed. Either way he couldn't get it open.

He hit the window with his fist. "Katherine! Katherine!" he yelled. For a second he thought he saw her eyelids flutter, then…nothing. "Katherine!" he yelled again, the sound absorbed by the dense snow.

He looked around for something to smash the window with, and failing that, he hurried back up the slope to his truck. He found a crowbar and returned as fast as he could to the car. As he neared it, he lost his footing and fell facedown in the snow. Getting back to his feet, he made it to the car and swung the crowbar down hard on a rear side window, shattering the glass into myriad of shards.

He found the lock switch, tugged it up, then dropped the crowbar on the back seat. He grabbed the front door handle and it opened. Finally he could touch Katherine. He felt her throat, found her pulse, and his relief was overwhelming. "Katherine, it's okay. I'm here. I'm here," he repeated as he fumbled with the seat belt.

He eased her back, saw that the blood on her face was from a small cut just above her eye. Nothing major. But her being unconscious scared him. He weighed his options. Leave her and get help, or take her up to his truck any way he could. The decision was an easy one. He wasn't leaving her again.

He managed to get her out of the car, lifting her into his arms, then he began the long, hard climb back to the truck. He kept going, even when he thought he couldn't, and after what seemed like forever, he was on the road. Another car was there, Carl and Dave in the tow truck. "Kenny, what in hell? Someone called and said your truck was blocking the road."

"Accident," Mac said, carrying Katherine toward the man's truck. "The hospital. Get me there as fast as you can."

"Sure, sure," Carl said, coming around to help Mac to the tow truck. He assisted him up into the cab with Katherine, then turned and yelled, "Dave, get Kenny's truck. Drive back to the garage, and I'll call you."

Dave headed for the truck still idling in the middle of the road as Mac sat with Katherine cradled in his arms in the tow truck. Carl climbed in behind the wheel and started down the road before he said anything. "Is she going to make it?"

He felt Katherine turn slightly into his chest, and he whispered, "She has to. She has to."

She moaned and his hold on her tightened. "I won't leave you. I won't leave," he whispered.

KATE AWOKE SLOWLY, through a softness that was all too inviting. She could just stay there, in never-never land, where she didn't have to feel or think, or be alone and never come back. But no matter what she tried, that slipped away from her. She had to wake up; she had to start feeling.

She lay very still, no idea where she was, the physical pain off at a distance behind a wall of grayness, but what happened with Mac was there. It was all there. She gasped softly at the pain and rawness of what she was feeling.

"Katherine?"

Her name. Mac staying it? No, that wasn't possible. She was delusional, her need making her crazy. Crazy, edgy, painful, needy. Love? Natty had been right. There was no rosy cloud to sit on with love.

Then someone touched her, a gentle touch on her cheek, fingers fleetingly brushing her skin, and the touch was remembered from the past. Mac. But the next touch on her arm, at her wrist, fingers pressed there, was not Mac's. It was efficient, testing, not comforting. Then a voice that she didn't know. "Good, very good. She's coming around."

"Thank God."

Mac?

"No, no." Her voice was a mere rasp.

"Katherine? Open your eyes. Open them."

Mac. It was him. A dream? She tried to open her eyes, but they were so heavy it took all her strength. Bright light, achingly bright, then easing, and she managed to open them enough to see white. Snow? No, white walls. A utilitarian clock. Eleven o'clock. Day? Night? The smell of medicine. A hospital? She was in a hospital.

A hand took hers, holding it tightly, then a touch on her cheek again. Mac. A caress that was unsteady and the whispered voice saying her name. "Katherine."

She managed to turn slightly to the sound, and Mac was there, Mac with the dark shadow of a beard, his hair mussed as if raked by worried fingers. Mac, hazel eyes watching her. "Mac? Wh…what…?" Her throat was dry and as if he read her mind, a straw touched her parched lips. She sipped the coolness, swallowed. Then the straw was gone, and she looked up at Mac.

It was his hand holding her, his other hand softly stroking her bare arm. "Shh," he said softly. "Just rest."

"What…happened?"

"You had a small accident outside of town, but you're fine. Just a bump on the head. Some bruises from your seat belt. Nothing serious."

She remembered now. The snow, the sliding, the tree. But if it wasn't serious, why did he look so concerned. "Accident?"

"You were leaving," he said in a low voice. "The car skidded on the ice."

She was leaving. Yes, she was leaving. She had to leave. She couldn't be here, not with Mac. She couldn't go through the leaving again. She struggled to get up, to run like crazy, but Mac moved and then his hands were on her shoulders. She was weak beyond words and she sank back in the bed, tears starting to sting her eyes. "Why…are you here?"

"I made a promise."

"Promise?" Her head was starting to ache and she grimaced. "What…promise?"

"When I found you in the car, I promised to stay with you, to not leave you."

No, no. She didn't want him here. She didn't want him so close, then him turn and go. "I...I release you from your promise," she breathed.

He shook his head. "You can't."

Another man was there, and Mac moved away to let the doctor, a gray-haired, slender man in a lab coat, introduce himself as Dr. Peters. The doctor who was leaving the clinic. Retiring. She remembered. He smiled down at her. "You're one lucky lady. A bump on the head. I heard your car wasn't so lucky."

"When can I leave?"

"In the morning. I'll check on you first thing, and if everything's okay, I'll sign your release." He motioned behind him. "Mac will make sure you follow directions."

She closed her eyes and sensed movement, then Mac was speaking to her from close by. "When I found you in the car, I thought..."

She opened her eyes as his voice trailed off. He was sitting by the bed, his hands gripping the lowered side rail. Pain. His eyes held pain. No anger. Just that horrible edge of pain. "I tried to tell you," she said. "I tried."

"I know." He sat back, exhaling as he ran a hand roughly over his face. Those hazel eyes were on her again. "I talked to James. He told me everything, and I told him that any story he thought he had was off-limits."

She bit her lip. "He won't print anything."

"No, he won't," Mac murmured. He came closer,

leaning toward her, and touched her again. His hand covered hers clenched by her side

She tried to pull free of the contact, the feel of him unbearable to her at that moment. "I didn't tell him anything," she managed as his hold on her tightened. "I swear."

"I know. I know." He stared at her. "You could have been killed," he said in a gruff voice, his hold on her tightening. "You could have…" He exhaled, and without warning, he bent down and kissed her.

The touch was one thing. But the kiss? She thought she really would die of the pain. His kiss was all she wanted, then he was pulling back, but he was still very close. His hands moved to frame her face. "Don't leave me," he breathed. "Please, don't leave me."

"You, you told me to go. I…I never meant to hurt you. I never, never meant to hurt you or Tyler or Natty."

"Katherine, listen to me. I was wrong. I was dead wrong. I thought…" His touch on her trembled. "God, I've made such mistakes in my life, horrible mistakes. I won't make another and I won't take three months to figure this out."

"What?"

"Katherine, I love you. I've loved you forever. Before I knew a Katherine Ames existed, I loved you. And when I found you in that car…" He took an unsteady breath, and she realized that it wasn't pain she saw in his eyes, but fear. The same fear she had in her. The fear that she'd never be in Mac's world again. The fear that this love she felt was all she'd ever have of him. But now, he was saying things that were erasing that fear.

For a woman who never cried, never, never showed her emotions, the tears were there again. Tears of uncertainty and tears of hope. Yes, hope. "Oh, Mac."

"Come back to the ranch...just for a while We can talk, and we can make sense out of all this."

All the sense she had to make was that she loved him, and he'd said he loved her. That meant he must have forgiven her. Now if she could forgive herself...maybe there was hope. She'd never believed in hope, in happy endings, but for the second time in her life, she thought that maybe both were real. "You love me?" she asked, almost afraid to ask in case she'd been hallucinating when he'd said it the first time.

"Amazing, isn't it?" he said. That look was still there, the fear. And she reached out to him, touching his jaw with her fingertips, relishing the prickle of his new beard and the heat under it.

"Amazing," she echoed.

"Will you come back with me and let me convince you that I mean what I'm saying?"

"For how long?" she asked.

"As long as it takes," he said without hesitation.

"Forever?"

"What?"

"Forever?" she repeated on a whisper.

He was motionless. "Oh, yes. Forever."

"I'll come," she said.

"Why?"

She felt something in her thaw, some coldness she'd had all her life dissolving. The agony, and worry, and edginess, and pain. What Natty hadn't told her about was the glory. That easing in the soul. "Well, I don't have a job I have to get back to and…" He was frowning, the easing she felt not evident in him at all.

"Why?" he repeated.

She covered his hands on her face with hers, then said the raw truth. "Because I love you."

The kiss was instant and binding, deep and compelling, and forged a contract between the two of them. Forever. Mac was with her in the bed, pulling her into his arms, holding her, kissing her again and again. "I'm going to talk to the doctor and get you released tonight."

She snuggled into him. "He said the morning."

"I'll take care of you."

"Yes, Mac, you *are* a doctor. You need to practice medicine." She pressed her hand to his chest, felt his heart under her palm. "You can't waste that."

"You're right," he said, holding her more tightly to him. "I've been rethinking so much, so very much, and with Dr. Peters retiring, maybe Natty was right. Maybe I could take over here."

She pushed back, looking at him in the bed by her. "Would you do that?"

"Yes," he said, his smile a wonder to behold. "If I can, I will."

"That's wonderful."

"What about you?"

She patted his chest. "I'm fine."

"No, your writing?"

She settled back by him. "I'll figure that out. I can get a job at the newspaper. You have one around here, don't you?"

"A weekly, which I'm sure could use a good reporter. Anything has to be better than stories on whose cow got loose."

She laughed softly. "I could do that."

"Sure, you could make the damn cow talk, too, but what I was thinking about was you writing your novel, and in between, you could freelance. Your first story could be about me for your old boss."

"What?"

"I've been thinking that sooner or later, someone's going to do it, and if I give them enough to make them stop wondering, they'll lose interest and leave us alone. I'd rather you wrote it than anyone else. Besides, there'll be plenty of time to collaborate after we get married."

"Married?"

He was grinning again. "Did you think I was asking you to be a boarder at the ranch or to just plain live in sin?" He shifted, facing her. "I want it all. I want you and marriage. I want a future." His smile faltered and his voice grew lower and a bit unsteady. "That's the first time I've ever asked anyone to be my future."

"It's the first time I was ever asked to be anyone's future." She could barely get out the words. "I love you and I promise I'll love you for the rest of my life."

"I'll hold you to that promise."

Epilogue

Six months later

THE SEARCH FOR MAC PARISH IS OVER

Dr. Mackenzie Parish, known as "doctor to the Stars" in Los Angeles, dropped out of sight a year and a half ago amid rumors and innuendoes. The axium that "you can't go home again," has been disproved by Parish, who went home to a small ranching community in Montana.

What started as a trip back to Bliss, Montana, for a family emergency when his younger brother, Michael, and his wife, Janice, were killed in a single-car accident became a permanent relocation for Parish. He traded the bright lights and fast lane of L.A., for a small private medical practice and the overseeing of the family's ranch. He is settling in with his new wife, Katherine Ames, a journalist from Los Angeles, and his brother's son, Tyler.

Mac scanned the rest of the article as he stood in the kitchen, then read the last line. ''Dr. Mackenzie Parish is home,'' and under that was the by-line, ''Katherine Ames-Parish.'' He closed the most recent issue of the *Final Word* and was startled when Katherine spoke from right behind him.

''You're back,'' she said, and he turned to find her inches from him, in jeans, white tank top and barefoot, looking at the magazine in his hands. ''Well? How is it?''

He set it down on the kitchen table. ''Brilliant.''

''I kept it simple in the tag to the story. Just enough information to satisfy them, but I didn't go into a lot of detail.'' She smiled at him. ''Just, 'Parish and Katherine Ames, former features reporter for this magazine, were married in a New Year's Eve ceremony on his ranch in front of a small group of family and friends,' and that was it. I think it was just enough.''

He framed her face with his hands. ''Just enough. I think they'll leave us alone now.''

''Wonderful,'' she breathed.

He wanted her. It was that simple. He'd been gone all morning and that was way too long. ''I left Debra in charge of the clinic. No one's in crisis.'' He looked past her. ''I take it that the boy's not in jeopardy or jeopardizing anyone else?''

''You have it right,'' she said, rising on tiptoe to kiss him lightly. Suddenly she seemed hesitant. ''Can we talk?''

"Is something wrong? Did you hear from Borneo?" He still couldn't get over the fact that her parents hadn't come here for the wedding. That they hadn't even sent a card.

"Actually they're in India now, but it's not about them. I just want to talk to you," she said.

He didn't hesitate. "Natty," he called without looking away from his wife. "Could you keep an eye on Tyler for a while?"

"No problem," she called back from the front of the house. "Take your time. We're building the Eiffel Tower."

"She is always so good about watching him," Katherine said. "And she never asks why we have to go out to the stable, or get away."

"She understands," he said.

"Good. Where can we talk?"

He smiled at her. "How about being traditional this time and use the bedroom?"

Her color deepened and he loved that about her. She blushed so easily and it only made her look lovelier. "Sure, the bedroom," she said, and took his hand, her fingers curling around his. He hoped that he never got used that jolt of awareness when she touched him, just putting her hand in his.

"I love you," she said. "I really do."

"That's a coincidence," he said. "I love you."

He drew her to him, meaning to kiss her quickly, to tide him over until they got behind closed doors. But the passion exploded between them, and the next thing he knew, they were clinging to each other in the middle of the kitchen, and he was barely able to breath, let alone think straight.

It was Katherine who drew back, saying, "The bedroom?"

Going ten feet seemed a long way right then, but he nodded. "Yes, the bedroom," he said, then lifted her into his arms. "The better to get there sooner," he explained.

She snuggled into him, silent until they were in the bedroom. He let her go long enough to shut the door and lock it, then she was in his arms, and nothing else mattered in the world. He took her in a rush, a frenzy of need, that was echoed in her. And this time, like every time they came together this way, something between them was strengthened, a sureness that this was forever was forged.

Lying on the bed, whispering together, that sureness grew even more. "Okay, now we can talk," he breathed against her hair as she snuggled into his side.

She spread her hand on his bare stomach and he felt his body start to tense again. Then she raised herself on her elbow, her hair tangled around her slightly flushed face. "Mac, I know that—"

"There's something wrong, isn't there," he said.

"Mac, what do you think about this, the family and everything? Are you sure it's what you really want?"

"You have to ask?"

Her fingers touched his chin, and they were less than steady. "I just wasn't sure, and I know that we haven't really talked about Tyler and him being…well, sort of, an only child and…'' She bit her lip. ''Oh, Mac, it was an accident. But I sure hope you aren't upset about it.''

''Accident?'' he repeated, then saw it in her eyes. ''You…you're…we're going to have a baby?''

She nodded, and the joy he thought he couldn't surmount after marrying Katherine and having her in his life grew beyond all reason. ''Yes, I'm pregnant. Six weeks or so, it seems.''

''You and your accidents,'' he said unsteadily as he reached for her. ''God, I love you and your accidents.''

With his beautiful wife pregnant with his child, Mac realized that he'd finally found himself. And in the process, he'd found the only real home he had in this world. In Katherine's arms. Yes, Dr. Mackenzie Parish was home.